THE LONG WAY AROUND

Ryan S. Pack

ISBN-13: 978-0-9860-564-4-4

This collection is dedicated to several people: Melissa Fry, my first outside-the-family editor, my brothers- in-arms, for many a night of deep thought, undying dedication, and vast inebriation, and lastly, to my grandmother, Bebe Pack, for simply being herself, a feat no mere mortal could have ever managed. The man I am today is thanks to each of you in different ways, so it's all your fault when I go sideways and blow up the planet.

(Chew on that in the dark of night.)

Contents

Foreword

Foreword

Sometimes you find yourself in the middle of a story you're writing and you suddenly realize that it's going to end a page or two from where you are. This can be pretty disconcerting at times, because you further realize that the story you're writing, while it may be good in and of itself, is in no way long enough to be a novel or a novella. Enter that comforting little subdivision of writing called the short story. There are many folks out there that will tell you that short stories are a waste of time, but then again, there are many folks out there that believe the lunar landings were done in a Hollywood studio under the strictest secrecy, so you can be the judge of that.

I started writing short stories when I was a young man, seventeen or eighteen; somewhere in that neighborhood, but most of them were… well, in a word, crap. And so they were summarily pitched into the fire. After some time, I got the knack for writing short stories (now, how good they are, well that's up to you to decide), and I wrote several, just for my own pleasure. I never felt the urge to push a story further than it should go, to pad it out into a novel, because sometimes, the stories just end, folks, no matter what the writer's opinion may be. Whenever I say that to someone they look at me like I've got broccoli sprouting out my ears, but that doesn't change the fundamental truth of my statement. Everyone seems to think that, as the author, I am God in that little particular universe, and in a way, I guess I am. But I can tell you from the heart that I hope that God doesn't approach our universe the same way I approach mine. Because if He/She/It/Them does, we're all sunk. When I sit down and start writing, I haven't a clue how it's going to turn out. I rarely keep any notes of story ideas, I just sit down and let 'er rip, and then sit back and see what happens.

The short story, to me, is just about the most beautiful thing in writing. It doesn't eat up vast amounts of time, either in the writing or the reading. It encapsulates a story in a neat little form, and then zips it out for consumption. The eleven short stories that follow cross a pretty large chunk of my life. The first, "The Road to Bifrost", was written in 1990, and the last, "The No-Fun Club", was written in 2014. For those of you that are counting, that's twenty-four years. My first short story is old enough to buy beer, by Odin! How the hell did that happen?

I find myself drifting off on a tangent, something that is fun at parties, not so much fun in literature. As I was saying at the beginning of this little missive, you can sometimes find yourself in the middle of a story and have the thing just slam head-on into a brick wall, leaving you befuddled, to say the least. But once you get over that initial shock, and you read what you have written, more times than not you will find that where the story ended was exactly where it needed to. I find it difficult to not get in there and change this paragraph, or insert this sentence, but for the most part I just listen to that slightly threatening voice in the back of my head that says, "Leave it be or I'll break your damn fingers." I'm not completely sure if my subconscious packs a big enough wallop to follow through with that threat, but I ain't about to find out, thank you very much.

I hope you enjoy reading these stories as much as I did writing them. If you don't…well, that's cool too, because I'm gonna keep right on writing them until it bores me. I've tried to "cull the herd" on this collection, and only add stories that I thought were up to par. If I have failed to do so, and these all stink, then I must admit that I didn't write

the first one of these pieces of crap, it was all my evil twin's fault. I'll

find that bastard one day, oh yes, he can't hide forever…

<u>She Saw</u>

One

She saw him walking down the hallway of the high school that, up until that moment, she had no idea they shared. Sitting on a bench with one of her friends, she glanced down the hallway and was taken aback. For a moment, she lost the ability to breathe. Standing in the hall, his hand raised to one of his friends, was the man she would marry. He was standing under a skylight, and the sun danced off his curly blonde hair, giving it the appearance of spun gold. The moment lasted only seconds, but as time came slamming back like a gale force wind, she was able to draw a sharp breath. She turned to her friend and asked if she might know the boy she had just seen. Her friend gave her an odd little smile and told her that yes, she knew him, he was her cousin. The girl grinned and told her friend that one day, she would be in the family. She stood and marched purposefully down the hall to inform this boy that he was the love of her life and that one day, they would be together forever...

Two

She saw him stomping mud from his boots as he left the field, surrounded by short, furry Highland cattle, all of which seemed to vie for his time. He gave one a good-natured slap on the rump and sent it on its way. The sun had broken through the clouds for just a moment, and the sullen rain gave way to a bright beam of light the traversed the field on where he stood, staring off to the north at the snow-capped peak of Ben Nevis. She drew her shawl tightly around herself and gave a small gasp as he turned and started back down the glen. He threw his plaid over his shoulder and strode towards the low stone fence at the bottom of the glen. The sun dappled its light onto his unbound hair, which the wind raised in a mantle around his head, the light shining through it and creating a golden halo. She set her shoulders and began walking towards him. Propriety be damned, this was the boy with whom she would grow old and die. He just didn't know it yet...

Three

She watched him hand out bits of chocolate to the children of the village, a large, silly grin on his face. She sat in the shade of the small outbuilding that faced the road, one of the few buildings in the village that bore no scars of battle. Her friends sat with her, looking at the group of soldiers in the village square, some with trepidation, some with open hostility, and still others with simple apathy. As she watched, the soldier took off his helmet and wiped his brow clear of sweat. His rifle was slung across his back, and his green fatigues were covered with mud and grime. He slid his dog tags off his neck and dangled them in front of a chubby toddler, laughing with the child as it grabbed at the shiny metal. His gaze traveled upward and for the briefest of moments, his blue eyes met her green ones. She heard herself take a sharp inward breath. He smiled and nodded to her. His sweat dampened hair was caught in an errant breeze, and a few curls lifted from the top of his head. The sun shone through these with diffuse, golden light. She rose from her seat and, ignoring the outcries of her companions, walked towards him. They would snub her for this, she knew, but it was of no matter. The fact that she spoke not a word of English was of no matter, either. She would hope this American boy knew enough German to converse with her, and if not, she would just have to learn enough of his language to tell him that he was to be her husband, for now and for always...

Four

She looked across the town square at the men and boys resplendent in their grey uniforms. Some of the boys were barely in their teens, and these glanced about nervously at the officers, so sure and proud on their mounts. She walked down the street, carefully avoiding the mud churned up by the past night's rain and the passage of so many horses. She smiled sweetly at the soldiers from under her umbrella, as she had been instructed by her parents to do. These were the boys that were going to end Northern aggression and save their way of life, and they were to be shown friendship and respect. The war was an abstract concept for her, something to read about in the papers, so far from home. She made her way past the knot of soldiers in the square, each checking and rechecking equipment and arms, and was nearly to her destination at the General Store when a shadow fell across her path. Looking up, she beheld a young soldier in a mismatched uniform, a quail feather stuck rakishly into his hat. With a smile, he doffed his hat and said simply, "Ma'am", before stepping politely out of her way. Her umbrella fell slack to her side as she stared into the eyes of the young man before her. His eyes, blue as the sky, disappeared when he smiled, and his tousled blonde hair fell across his forehead. He flipped it back from his brow, and the sun shone through it like gold. He stepped past her and rejoined his unit in the square. She knew then that she would learn this boy's name, and that he would court her when this war had ended, for he was hers and she his, even if he was unaware of it. She quickened her step and turned towards to courthouse to find the recruitment officer and her future husband's name...

Five

She moved with haste through the cobbled streets, anxious to
return home before the city began to fill with spectators from all the
outlying provinces. The city would be in a complete uproar for the next
week, she knew, and the safest place for a young, unmarried girl during
such a time was at home with her family. Although her father had
given strict instructions that she be back from the market before
midday, her desire to view the spectacle of the Triumph warred with
her wish to not disappoint her father. From the direction of the Plaza,
she could hear the swelling sound of voices, raised in jubilation. A
quick look, she thought, just from the edge of the crowd. She changed
direction and moved towards the wall of sound. She was nearing the
back of the crowd when, from a side alley, rough hands grabbed her
and drew her into the darker recesses within. Coarse men, roughened
even further with drink, pawed at her, making obscene remarks. She
turned this way and that, vainly trying to find escape. The men,
emboldened by her fear, began to pull at her clothing more forcefully.

One man, who seemed to be the leader of this mob, stepped forth and grabbed her by the hair, shoving her against the wall. She closed her eyes as tears ran freely down her cheeks. She steeled herself for what she knew was to come when she heard a choked gasp. Opening her eyes, she stared straight into the face of her would-be attacker, his eyes bulging out in terror, his hands throw wide. Looking down, she saw in amazement that a gladius was poised firmly across the man's throat. Following the gladius, she saw the arm and the Legionnaire to which it was attached standing calmly next to her. With a jerk of his head, he sent the men in the alley scurrying out into the crowd. With a smile, the man nodded his head to her and sheathed his sword. He turned to walk away, but was stopped when she placed her hand on his arm. He turned back to her, and seeing the fear still in her eyes, smiled and offered his arm to her. His blue eyes were warm and friendly, and with a flourish, he took off his helm, and bowed deeply before her. His blonde hair picked up highlights in the afternoon sun. He must have been of Celtic stock, to be colored so. She smiled back, and as they walked out of the alley together, she knew that this man was to be her husband, and that this very night, her father would welcome his new son into their home...

Six

She saw… and still sees.

A Question of Humanity

One

The roar of the crowd was a physical wave that pulsed and ebbed over him. Even at this range, he thought. My God, how can the people there stand it? He was on a small hill with a copse of ash and oak trees on either side of him, providing him cover. Not that he needed that much cover, for the Ghillie suit constructed for him by a U.S. Marine made him all but invisible even to a man standing less than a foot away. He took a steadying breath and stared down the scope of the Barrett M82 .50 BMG sniper rifle, settled rock-steady on its bipod. The scope, a Leupold Mark IV ER/T, at 25X, made the target standing almost a mile away look about the size of the action figures he had played with as a child. He closed his eyes for a moment and focused on his breathing.

When he opened them again he looked again at his target. The feeling of unreality surged through him again, as it had all morning. He took another shuddering breath and drank a sip of water from the Camelbak hydration system on his back. *Nothing but the best technology has to offer for this*, he thought. He considered eating a protein bar, as he had skipped breakfast to be here well before dawn. All the training he had undergone told him this was a mistake, that there should be no unnecessary movement on his part. Then he realized that the men charged with security of the target wouldn't be able to see him if he jumped up and down, not at this range. Hell with it, he thought, I'm hungry.

As he munched on the tasteless but filling protein bar, he checked his watch. He had plenty of time. The target wouldn't even take the podium for his speech for another half-hour. He wanted to make his shot at exactly the right second. Nothing was left to chance, not this time. This was too important. Documents had been studied, and then re-studied, time-tables consulted; weather patterns discerned… no variable left to fate. As he finished his body-fueling food, he considered what had brought him to this point, as he has a thousand times before.

His name was Adam Carriage, and he was twenty-seven years old. He was not a soldier by trade, although he had spent a great deal of time with them over the last two years. Hanging out in bars just off military bases, he had grown accustomed to the sounds of military

jargon. He had studied all the acronyms that came so fluently from the

mouths of these warriors, a code that to a civilian sounded as foreign as

Greek. Within a few months, with a burr haircut and some

personalized dog tags he had ordered off-line, he was able to strike up

a conversation with any soldier that walked into a bar just about

anywhere in the Continental United States. Many, many beers later, talk

would turn to weapons of war and their usages. There were no

shortages of soldiers with hands-on experience with these weapons,

with wars raging in Iraq and Afghanistan. He found it particularly

disappointing that he was unable to find any snipers in these bars, for

these were the men he most wanted to speak with. After several

conversations with the other soldiers, he found that snipers most often

drank alone, or with other snipers. They were seen as a different sort of

soldier, closer to an executioner than a regular soldier.

Adam was persistent, however, and within a few months was

able to locate a Marine Force Recon Scout Sniper that had just

returned from Iraq to North Carolina. He was sitting in a squalid bar

with lousy lights and even lousier music when Adam walked in. He

picked out that the man was a jarhead from the moment he walked in, and grabbed a stool about three places down from the man. The Marine looked up from his whiskey and nodded to Adam. He nodded back and said "Semper Fi.". The Marine grinned blearily and replied in the same manner. After a few more drinks, Adam offered to by the Marine a beer. The Marine gratefully accepted.

"Where you from, Marine?" asked Adam.

The man smiled drunkenly and said, "Everywhere, little brother, everywhere."

Adam grinned back and said, "You just back from downrange?"

The Marine nodded, stuck his hand across and introduced himself. "Lance Corporal Marcus Rheingold, U.S.M.C. Born and raised in Loosy-anna. What's you're handle?"

As he had practiced countless times before, Adam replied "Jeff Carson, straight outta the sticks. Pembroke, West Virginia. Just joined the Green Machine last year. Got outta Parris Island, and now I'm lookin' to find me some way of making it into S.T.A."

Rheingold looked almost comically surprised. "Are you shitting me?"

Adam, looked surprised and said, "Fuck, no, I'm not shitting you. My old man said that Surveillance and Target Acquisition was the way to go. Force Recon, man. Fuck that spray and pray bullshit, I wanna see what I'm hitting."

Rheingold took a long pull on his beer and wiped the foam from his upper lip. "Well, Private Carson, it just so happens that you are drinking beer with a Marine Force Scout Sniper."

Adam laughed. "Right", he said, "and President Bush is your college buddy."

Rheingold looked grim. "I ain't lyin' boy. I just spent eighteen months in Shittown, with a BMG in my hand."

Adam looked suitably impressed. "No shit, for real?"

"Goddamn right, for real."

"Fuck me", Adam breathed. "I'm all lined up. Just gotta finish six months for my MOS 0321 billet and I'm golden."

Rheingold looked at Adam carefully. When he finally spoke, his words were barely audible. "Be sure this is what you want, man. The shit over there… it fucks with a man. Don't get me wrong, I love the Corps, but… well, just be sure."

The rest of the conversation fell along those same lines. As the evening drew to an end, Adam and Rheingold exchanged numbers, with the promise that Rheingold would give Adam a little prep before he left for his training. After three weeks, Adam was familiar with all manner of things to do with sniping. Adam purchased a .50 BMG, telling Rheingold that he had a friend whose father owned one and had allowed him to borrow it, just to get used to it. That day, Rheingold showed Adam the finer points of the weapon, and within two more weeks of practice, was able to place a three-inch group at fifteen hundred yards out in a man-sized target. "Remember", Rheingold had told him," There are 1760 yards in a mile. So, at 1500, you've got just shy of that. Everything I've told you, you gotta remember, right down to the millimeter." Adam then had Rheingold help him construct a Ghille suit, which blended so well with the local flora that he was impossible to see, even feet away. Rheingold heralded Adam's successes, telling him that he was a sure thing to make it into S.T.A.

Adam, however, had other plans.

With a twinge of sadness and guilt at his ruthless use of an honest man, Adam left North Carolina and traveled to his compound in Nevada. There, he practiced with his rifle daily, until he was able to place his shot exactly where he wanted it at exactly 1650 yards away, regardless of windage. The rest of the time, Adam spent reading background material on his target. His compound was a lavish affair, nothing Spartan about it. He trained his body in his state-of-the-art weight room. He spent several hours a day practicing German. He was soon fluent, with a touch of Bavarian in his accent. Nothing was left to chance, nothing overlooked. He hired the best tailors to make him suits of clothing, down to the undergarments, from the 1930's. He purchased watches, rings, cufflinks, and all other manner everyday items, either from or exactly replicated from that same era. Papers were duplicated, using photo manipulation software. Thank God money is no object, he thought wryly.

After all, it wasn't every day you got the chance to assassinate Adolph Hitler.

Adam Carriage was a time-jumper.

Two

He lay on the ground now, 1600 yards away from the Nuremberg Nazi rally party, just east of Regensburgerstraße. It was Monday, September 13th, 1937. Adam had been lying there for hours and hours, but he was a patient man by nature. He knew that Hitler would be giving a speech during the closing ceremony of the Party Congress, and it was at that exact moment, when Hitler was at his most fervent, the thousands massed at their zenith of adulation, that Adam intended to place a single, well-aimed .50 bullet directly through "Der Führer's" hate-ridden, evil heart. Adam smiled at the thought of thousands of screaming Nazis suddenly silenced at the spectacle of their glorious leader's heart exploding from his chest.

He waited.

Nothing had been left to chance.

As the time for his shot approached, he began to feel his nerves tingling. He didn't allow this to upset him. It was natural to feel nervous when you were about to change the course of human history forever, he thought. He looked at his hand. The minute quiver seemed grossly magnified. Can't have this, he thought. Not at this range. I'll fuck up and send the shell into that frigging Swastika behind the bastard. He slowly moved his hand down into a pouch on his belt. In it was a small syringe filled with liquid Valium. He had measured the dosage exactly for this eventuality. With a slight hiss of pain, he jammed the syringe into his arm and waited. Within a few moments, he grew calm. Not stuporous, just very, very calm. He looked at his hand again. It was steady.

He looked through his spotting scope and watched the Nazi banners flutter in the wind, then adjusted his scope accordingly. He drew a deep breath and let it out. Closing one eye, he sighted down the scope. The image of Adolph Hitler sprang into his view like a demonic marionette. The man was gesturing wildly, pounding the podium as he roared into the microphones. Adam could almost make out his words over the P.A. system. Although Hitler was flailing his arms about, he did not move his body much. This suited Adam just fine. At this range,

Hitler could bend over and pick up a piece of paper after Adam fired, and still have time to stand back up before it hit, provided that he stood back in exactly the same place. Another check for the windage, another minute adjustment, and Adam was ready. He settled the crosshairs on the center of Hitler's chest and began slowly squeezing the trigger. In the next five seconds, he thought, I will have saved countless millions of lives.

"No, you won't", growled a voice from directly behind him. Adam, muttered a stifled scream, and rolled to the left, drawing the SIG .40 Automatic from his hip holster as he did so. As the sights settled on this new target, it occurred to him that the voice had replied in English, not German, and that it had replied to a statement made only in his mind!

Standing before him in the shade of a tree stood a sepulchral figure, his clothing ragged, his face scarred and gaunt. Adam lay on his back, the pistol in his hands leveled at the man. He looked strangely familiar. Adam finally found his voice and spoke.

"You've got about three seconds to convince me you aren't a hallucination, or I'm going to put a bullet through your head, just to be safe."

The man laughed, a cold and bitter sound. "A rather odd way of committing suicide, don't you think?" he said.

It struck Adam like a physical blow as he realized that he was staring at a horribly mangled and older version of himself. He stared, speechless, at the figure before him, trying to make sense of it. This had never happened before, although he had hypothesized that it could, in theory. Jumping through time to view himself had seemed a bit bizarre to him, and he had never done it.

"It is bizarre, and I don't like doing it, either", the man replied to Adam's unspoken thought.

A small sound escaped Adam's throat. "What the fuck?" he whispered.

The man grinned down at him. "Yeah, I know this is very strange for you. Believe me; it's strange for me, too. I don't know how this is going to turn out, and it freaks me out a little."

Adam finally found his voice again. "What the hell are you doing here?"

The man sighed and looked forlornly out across the vast distance towards the rally. "It's all so strange. I remember all of this, right up to the point that I jumped here. I don't remember having this conversation with you, though, so I know that the future is still up for grabs. It's all so odd." Suddenly, he looked back at Adam, his eyes hard as granite. "Take your rifle and jump. Now. Go back to the compound. Live your life, and leave the past alone. You have no idea what you are doing."

Adam was aghast. "What the hell do you mean, I don't know what I'm doing?" he asked incredulously. "I'm averting World War Two, goddammit! I'm saving millions of innocent lives!"

The man shook his head sadly. "Yes, that is true; you would save millions of lives if you kill that fucker. However, you will also end billions of lives if you do it. Believe me, I know. I've seen it. You have to trust me. Take the rifle and jump. Go home and leave this shit alone."

Adam looked around confusedly. He couldn't get a handle on this. All he knew for certain was that the target he had spent several years training for was almost done with his speech and about to leave the podium. He looked again at the gaunt man. "Look", he said, "I don't know what kind of bullshit this is, but I've got no time for it. You take one step towards me, I'll blow your damned brains out. I'm here to kill that mass-murderer, and that's by-God what I'm going to do. Stand clear." He turned back towards his rifle. The man behind spoke again, his voice low and urgent.

"Listen, dammit, you can't shoot him. If you pull that trigger, you will doom the whole planet to a thousand years of darkness. You have to trust me. I know it sounds ridiculous, but if events aren't allowed to happen the way they are supposed to, you'll destroy all that is good on this Earth!"

Adam grunted in disgust. "Right. By killing the most infamous monster of all time, I'll fuck up all that is good on earth. Makes sense to me." He sighted back down his rifle.

The man tried once more, his voice becoming even more plaintive.

"When you killed Hitler in 1937, you're right, World War Two didn't happen. At least, not the way it was supposed to. It wound up being a much smaller affair, with fewer countries involved, and it only lasted a little over a year, but that's not the point! Hitler has to live! When you killed him, the Final Solution never took place!"

Adam turned from his rifle. "Well, no shit, Sherlock, why do you think I'm doing it? What happened to you? Have you gone insane or something? Great future I seem to have. Asshole." He turned back to the rifle again.

"Yes, goddammit!" shouted the man. "I am halfway insane! We all are! The whole world! If you kill that man, you will stop something that has to happen! The Final Solution was a horrid, atrocity, I grant you that, but there was a reason for it! Not the Jews, not the homosexuals, not the dissidents, none of that. That was terrible. But Hitler killed more than the Jews in those camps! In 1942, at Auschwitz, the S.S. murdered a boy, a Gypsy boy from Romania. That boy was supposed to die there! He could not live! He cannot live! For the love of God, Adam, if you kill Hitler, you will save the life of the child that grows up to become the Antichrist!!!"

Adam looked over his shoulder. "My God, you really are crazy. Get the fuck away from me. Do it now." He looked back down the scope. Hitler was giving his final salute to the masses. Adam began squeezing the trigger again. From behind him, he heard the man's voice softly say: "This is why I don't remember how it ends. God's mercy on us both."

Adam heard the click of the cocking gun. He began to roll, but the movement was lost in the sound of thunder. The whole world seemed to be on fire. Gasping blood into the cloudless blue sky, he thought, What's happening? I can't feel my...

Darkness. The void.

Three

Adolph Hitler strutted away from the podium and towards the open Mercedes that would ferry him back to Berlin. There was so much to do in the coming year. He smiled blissfully as he stared at the passing scenery.

So very much to do.

Conversation with the Devil

"Hi, there."

"I was wondering if I could have just a minute or two of your time. No, I'm not giving a survey, or selling anything. It's nothing like that. I just want to speak with you for just a moment. That okay? Good."

"First off, please allow me to introduce myself…"

"Sorry, inside joke. It kills me. Again, I'm truly sorry. Won't happen again."

"What? Why, yes, I do have a pleasant laugh, don't I? Thank you for noticing."

"Now, where was I? Oh, yes, introductions. I am the Devil."

"No, it's not French! What are you, some kind of moron?"

"Okay, you're right; I didn't mean to say that. That was offensive. No, I mean I am the Devil. Lucifer, Beelzebub, Satan. Follow me?"

"I can see from the look in your eyes that you don't. Okay, a small demonstration, then."

"Yes, that was impressive, wasn't it? The wings are mine by birth, but the horns...well, that was kind of a little practical joke by God. He's a funny guy."

"Anyway, have we established that I am, in fact, the Devil? Good. By the way, you're taking all this remarkably well."

"Oh. Well, that many beers would be a factor, I suppose."

"Anyway, back to the point. I'd like to talk to you for a bit, try to explain things to you from my point of view, if that's all right. See, I've always been presented in a somewhat bad light. Prince of Darkness, Father of Lies... you know, that old chestnut. I'm not really that bad of a guy once you get to know me. There are just a few things I'd like to clear up about me and my situation. You know, just so the world can get a well-rounded view of things before they go off all half-cocked making decisions based on a single side of the story. See, I'm the sort of guy that..."

"Well, yes, you have a point there. I never thought of that. Well, I'm not looking for a prophet, per se, so I don't think that your status as town drunk will factor in all that much. One vote at a time, and all that. Besides, you can just tell your drinking buddies, who in turn will tell their drinking buddies and so forth. It'll all work out in the end."

"Now, as I was saying, I'm the kind of guy that needs to be shown something before I believe it. I should have been born in Missouri. I take nothing at face value. I like to check things out for myself, you know? That's what led me to my little tussle between myself and God."

Now, before you go off with any half-assed assumptions that I hate God, let me set you straight right off the bat. I love Him. He loves me. He is, after all, my Father. And by father, I don't really mean it in the "Our Father, who art in Heaven" sense of the word. I mean it more along the lines of "Hey Dad, can I borrow the car this weekend?" type of thing. He's my Dad, my Pops, my Old Man. Get me? Let me give it to you like this: It's like the father that went to Law School, set up a lucrative practice, and made a ton of cash. He did all this with one thing in mind: His son would follow along in his footsteps. All his

effort, his toil, has been bent on that one purpose. And the son doesn't

disappoint him; he's the B.M.O.C., college-prep all the way. Plays ball,

helps old ladies across the street, the works. A straight 4.0 G.P.A.

through school, a shoo-in for Valedictorian. Basically the best kid a

parent could ask for. But then, the night of his son's high school

graduation, here sits Dad. He's got all these ivy-league college

pamphlets lying on the coffee table in front of him, trying to imagine

which one his boy will choose. Visions of glory run rampant through

his mind, the father-son law firm already a reality to him. In walks the

Prodigal Son. He's shaved his head and joined the Marines. Now, you

can imagine how Dad reacts to that. He hits the roof, and a screaming

match ensues. Harsh words are exchanged, and in a fury, Dad orders

the son out of the house, never to return."

"There, I just described the war in Heaven you hear so much

about. No huge battles, no bloody conquests. Just a family brawl."

"What? Who, Michael? Ah, damn, it wasn't anything like that at

all. Mike's a great guy, but he's still my little brother, you know. Yeah, I

can just see Mike trying to cast me out of Heaven. He couldn't beat me at a game of Battleship, let alone throw me out of anywhere. He's a lot

different than all this crap people write about him. I mean, he's pretty

bad-ass, and if I wasn't who I am, I wouldn't want to piss him off. He's

actually quiet and kind of shy. That deal with the firstborn of Egypt,

man that really messed with his head for a long time, let me tell you.

But, no, the Archangel Michael didn't cast me out of anywhere. Yeah,

he was there when the fight went down, but he just kept his mouth

shut. What kid wants to get in the middle of a fight between their dad

and their older brother, you know?"

"So, anyway, there we were at the Gates of Heaven, me on one

side, God on the other, just giving each other the old Evil Eye bit.

Finally, God turns away and tells Michael to shut the gate. Mike does,

but just before it closes, he reaches out and touches my hand. I've

never forgotten that. Anyway, I take off with some friends of mine..."

"Hang on, hang on. I'm getting to that. Let me tell this story

my own way, will you?"

"Thank you. My friends and I head off for Earth, which is kind

of like Mardi Gras to us. This was back when you guys were still trying

to bash each other to death with rocks and pointed sticks, and you all looked like extras from a Jean Auel novel, you dig me? See, the whole

Big Fight between me and God stemmed from you. No, not you in

particular, you egoistical dummy, I mean humankind. God has what he

refers to as his 'Big Plan' when it comes to you guys, and He thinks

that if a bunch of Angels are traipsing about down here, we'll somehow

screw it all up. Now, I was pretty much used to doing just what He

asked of me, we all were. But like I said, I'm a curious guy. Once

something gets my attention, I've just got to check it out. I can't help it.

And, to be honest, if that is a sin, it's one that God hardwired into me,

now isn't it? He was pretty lenient with me the first few times he

caught me down here. He just gave me the standard lecture about not

messing around in the affairs of mankind. But the third or fourth time,

man, did He get some kind of pissed. You don't want to get God

pissed at you if you can help it. And we're talking a Charleston Heston

movie on meth kind of pissed. While He was ranting and raving about

how me being down here could 'Upset the delicate balance' and 'ruin

all the plans He had', it sort of just hit me like a thunderbolt. He didn't

really know what was going to happen! Now, don't get me wrong, if

He wanted to, He could tell you where every microbe is in the universe

this very second, and He could tell you where every microbe in the universe was a couple of million years ago. You get me? He knows everything that has happened, everything that is happening, but I don't think He knows everything that will happen. He could, if He wanted to, I'm almost positive about that. If He wanted to, I think he could give you a play-by-play of every single event that will take place from right now until whenever He decides to pull the plug on the whole thing. I'm just saying He doesn't want to be able to do that. Like he's blocked it from his mind. Let me put it this way, if you knew every single play of the Super Bowl, from beginning to end, would you still watch it? Well, yeah, you'd bet on it like hell, I don't doubt it, but would you watch it? I didn't think so. That's about what the deal is with God. He doesn't want to know everything that's going to happen so he won't get bored. Sounds pretty disappointing, doesn't it? Now, imagine how I felt. This was my Father, whom I had spent eons believing to be utterly omnipotent and infallible, and now I find out that He's leaving his greatest creation ever, Life, up to total chance. That was more than I could handle, and that's why I decided that if He could leave all this up for grabs, well, then I could come and go as I pleased down here. What difference would it make in the end, you know?"

"That's it. That's the Big Fight. That's why you guys have me down as the ultimate bad guy in all your texts, because I figure that since He didn't know what was going to happen, then there wasn't any chance of me screwing things up by hanging around."

"Sorry, I got just a bit long-winded there. I didn't mean to get so pissed, but it still bothers me. Anyway, here I am on Earth with all you fine folks. I watch you build civilizations that would have driven your ancestors completely off their collective rockers with the scope and scale of your buildings alone, and I watch you kill each other by the millions in the name of God, who, just remember, has left this whole shebang up to Fate. 'Free Will', He calls it. Bullshit, I call it. I have watched, just in the last century, mankind engulf this planet in not one, but two World Wars! I mean, come on, guys, get a damned clue! Quit killing each other for no reason!"

"You have, too! Don't tell me, Mister Man, I know damn well you killed Mrs. Abernathy from down the street in Williamsburg when you were a kid. Oh, natural causes, my ass! There's nothing natural about a heart attack brought on by some punk kid lighting M-80's under the window of an elderly lady!"

"Relax! Jeez, I'm not gonna run off and tell on you! Not my job. I'm just pointing out that you people do the weirdest shit imaginable. And I'm the bad guy! What a screwed-up situation. My point is, I'm tired of being portrayed as such an old meanie all the time, that's all. Give me a break. I don't have to hang out and listen to this abuse, you know. I could just pack up and go home."

"Hell? No such place, bub, unless you count this. Look, did I fail to explain my relationship with God to you clearly enough? He's my father, and like all sons and fathers, we fight occasionally. But then we get over it and move on. I've been back to Heaven millions of times since we had the Big One. God has decided that if I'm going to be so pig-headed about hanging out with the humans, He's just going to let me do it. I kind of wore him down, I guess you'd say. Or maybe He figures that I have a place in the fate of humanity, I dunno. I don't propose to know the mind of God. I may not like it, but I don't even think I can understand it. That would be blasphemy."

"Well, look, I've got to go. It's been nice talking with you. Remember what I said, I'm not such a bad guy. Tell your friends. See if maybe you can get something done about that pesky Bible of yours. It portrays me in a very unflattering light. Love one another, and try to get along. Worship God, and try to trust in Him. Nobody knows how hard that can be than I do, believe me. But hey! If I can do it, so can you guys. I'm out of here, pal. Take care of yourself, and I'll see you around,"

"Oh, and by the way, when you do check out (which is going to be sooner than later if you don't slow down on the Budweiser), there is one incredibly pissed off old lady by the name of Abernathy waiting to have a word with you. See ya!"

Culloden

ONE

"Oh, my God, honey!"

David Roberts turned towards his wife's breathless cry and smiled. Tamara was standing on a small knoll beside the walking trail, staring across the wooded valley at the castle and the grounds surrounding it. David smiled and raised his new digital camera. The cool, damp wind was blowing his wife's hair back from her face and she was clutching the heavy woolen tartan wrap, called an airsaid, she had bought at the gift shop nearby.

This is going to be the best picture I take this whole trip, he thought. He snapped several in rapid succession. The look of absent awe and joy on Tamara's face was plainly visible on the little viewscreen of his camera. The castle, with its stark while stone, stood out in sharp contrast against the dark, snow-capped mountains behind it. As David stood looking at his wife's profile in the steady wind, he was amazed to find his eyes misting. *Holy God*, he thought, *I think I just fell in love with her again*. If this is what the country had to offer, he was going to advise every troubled couple he knew to make reservations as soon as possible.

They had been on the brink of a divorce for longer than he cared to remember. Their children were grown and moved away, with Chris on the East Coast working in web design (whatever the hell that was), and Shelly in Alaska working as a marine biologist. Looking back, he considered that his rocky marriage to Tamara might have played a part in their children's decisions to move so far from their West Virginia home. They never said so, but David suspected.

With the children gone, the house had seemed to grow smaller instead of larger. He and Tamara avoided each other as much as possible, each seeming to realize that without the tempering influence of the children, the small squabbles could turn into marriage-ending wars at the drop of the hat. David was the Assistant County Attorney of Wise County, Virginia, and spent most of his time either in his office in town or at the courthouse. Tamara was on the board of the Wise County Historical Society, and was also active on the tourism board, as well. She was forever sporting a tourism pin that said "Welcome to

Wise County, The Safest Place On Earth!", the county motto. David considered it his job to keep Wise County that way.

This took care of their days, and they had learned the fine art of staying out of each other's way at night. David spent much of his night in his study, poring over files and watching television until he was certain that Tamara had gone up to bed, and then he would slip quietly into the kitchen and have a snack before retiring for the night in the bed in Chris' old room. This system seemed to work quite well in the ten months that had passed since Shelly had departed for Alaska, so it came as a shock one night in early spring when he turned his head from his computer screen to find his wife looking at him from the doorway.

"Why don't you go?" she asked, nodding her head towards the computer. "You've wanted to since before the kids were born."

David turned back to the screen. On it was the tourism homepage for Edinburgh, Scotland. He usually checked in on the going rates for plane tickets, car rentals, and the like at least once a month, and had for almost twenty years. It was more of a hobby, really. Tamara was right; he had wanted to go to Scotland since he was in his teens. It hadn't been feasible while he was in college, and with the coming of the children, he had always had too much to do any more than window shop.

"You've only got about a thousand years of vacation time coming to you", Tamara continued. "I don't think you've missed two days of work in the last ten years. We can certainly afford it now. So, go."

David, still staring at the screen, smiled slowly. What the hell, he thought, the worst thing she can do is say no, right? He turned back to her and said, "You're right, Tam. We can afford it, and I do have more than enough vacation time coming to me. I'll order tickets and book a hotel. The busy season hasn't really picked up over there yet, so there won't be a million other Americans over there, fucking things up and making it a crime punishable by death to be discovered to be a 'Bloody Yank'. I'll do it right now, tonight. One thing, though: I'm making reservations for two, or I'm not making them at all. What do you say?"

Tamara stared blankly at him for a moment, and then raised her hand to her throat, something she did whenever she was indecisive about something. After the moment grew pregnant with tension, David

had decided that there was no trip to Scotland in his future. With a

sigh, he turned back to the screen. Behind him, Tamara said, "Really?

You want me to come with you? Are you being serious, or what?"

David smiled again. "No, Tam", he said, "I'm pulling your leg.

I want to run off to Scotland and leave you here. You think I'm going

to give you free run of this place for a couple of weeks, only to find

you and Mark Preece curled up in bed, eating ice cream off each other's

nipples?"

Mark Preece was a nineteen year old boy from down the street

that had cut the Roberts' lawn over the previous summer. Tamara had

been watching him mow one summer afternoon when David had

walked into the kitchen. He had asked her what she was looking at.

Tamara had blushed to the roots of her hair, gave a nervous laugh and

left, mumbling something about making some lemonade. Later that

night she had confided to David that she was almost certain that Mr.

Mark Preece, with his Adonis good looks and his shoulder length

blonde hair, stuffed his shorts with tennis balls. Had to be stuffed.

Tamara flapped a hand at him and grinned. Color began to slowly creep up her throat and onto her face. "You dick", she said, now smiling openly. It occurred to David that Tamara hadn't smiled like that in a very, very long time.

He stood and walked over to her. He put his hands on her shoulders and looked into her eyes. "Yes, I'm being serious", he said. "You and me. Scotland. I think I still owe you that second honeymoon we always talked about. What do you say?"

Tamara ran her hand down the side of his face, coming to rest on the hollow of his throat. When she spoke, her voice was low and husky. "Make the reservations. It's late, and it's also bed time."

That night, David didn't sleep in Chris' bed.

<u>Two</u>

Now here they stood on the grounds of Castle Blair, northeast of Pitlochry They had been in the country for just over a week, and it had been like a fairy tale. They felt revitalized, and it seemed nothing could bring forth that old flame of resentment and anger between them. Even when their luggage was sent to Glasgow instead of Edinburgh, something that normally would have sparked a serious brawl, they just laughed about it and moved on.

David had rented a car and was doing all the driving. When he pulled out of the airport and began driving down the wrong side of the street, nearly wiping out another motorist, the man rolled down his window and shouted, "Wrong side. Yank! It's your other left!" Tamara had laughed so hard she began snorting like a feral pig. David grinned sheepishly and swerved into the proper lane, this time almost crushing an older man on a bicycle. The man's accent was so thick that David could barely make out one word in every three, but the sentiment was clear enough. David turned to his wife and asked, "Did that old man just call me a "fookin' bally-arsed tripe?" Tamara couldn't answer, only shaking her head helplessly; huge tears of laughter rolling down her face.

And that was how they got to Scotland.

They had seen about a thousand castles, it seemed, and visited the shores of every loch in Scotland. David had gone stag stalking in Perth, allowing Tamara time to do some shopping. They stayed in beautiful old Bed and Breakfasts, and awoke each morning looking forward to the day. They had visited the Glenmorangie distillery, and David had gotten too drunk to drive them back to the B & B they were staying that night. It was thirty miles to the B & B, and Tamara cursed him the entire way, gripping the steering wheel with fierce determination as she slowly made her way home. Driving down the wrong side of road was bad enough, she bitched, but the damn steering wheel is on the wrong side, too.

The days had melted into one another, and they had discovered that they actually enjoyed being together, something that surprised them both. The trip was nearing its end, and neither of them wanted to

see it go, so afraid that they might return to their old ways back home

and lose this new-found love for one another. They had only two days

left; Castle Blair today, and the battlefield of Culloden tomorrow. After

that, it was a drive back to the airport, a plane ride, and home.

They began to walk back to the castle, where they had parked

the car. The day was failing, and the clouds had broken up enough to

the west to allow the sun to lay broad stripes of orange and red across

the land. As they walked, hand in hand like a couple of high school

sweet hearts, Tamara began humming to herself. *This is going to be alright,*

she thought, *We were close to the edge there for a while, closer than I even want to*

admit, but this has made it all right again. She was very glad she had made

this trip. She was still lost in her pleasant thoughts when she was

suddenly pulled backwards, nearly falling to the ground.

David had come to a dead stop on the trail, and he had stopped

so suddenly, it had almost torn her arm out of socket. He stood stock-

still, facing northeast. His breath came out in little gasps.

"David? Honey, what's wrong?" Tamara asked. "Are you all right? Is it your heart?" Tamara was deathly afraid of heart attacks since one had carried off her father in the winter of 2001.

David didn't acknowledge her. He continued to stare intently at the darkening northern horizon. When he finally spoke, Tamara gave an involuntary cry; the voice coming out her husband's mouth sounded nothing like his usual quiet, clipped tone. Instead, it seemed as if he had eaten sandpaper, and his accent was so thick that Tamara could barely understand the words.

"Tha' damned Cumblerland wi' be comin' o'er to the moor by mornin', an' no mistake", he rasped. "We'll stand by tha true King, an' it take all we hae. I'll no' bend a knee to yon German popinjay than I'd cut my own heart out. There'll be a high spot o' killin' tae be done the morn, and myself plans on bein' in tha thick of it, aye. A day long to be remembered by kith and kin alike, Tha clans will no' be forced tae submit to some fat-arsed Sassenach, and him no' really even a true Sassenach, to boot!"

Tamara tried to pull her hand out of his grasp, but couldn't do it. His eyes had gone far away. Still thinking that he may be having a heart attack, or maybe a stroke, she began shaking him with her free

hand. "David! DAY-VID!!! This isn't funny! Are you all right?"

David gave an all-over body convulsion, and turned to face

Tamara. "Jesus, Tam, what the hell? You damn near pulled my arm

loose!"

She gave a sigh of relief. When she could muster the ability to

speak again, her voice was full of ice. "Very funny, fat man. I thought

you were having a heart attack, you ass!" David just stood there, trying

to figure out how he had managed to piss off his wife this time. When

Tamara spoke again, her voice was calmer and softer. "You've been

working on that accent, huh? You sounded pretty convincing."

David gave her a puzzled look. "What are you taking about?"

"The accent. You sound like you were born and raised here. I

didn't know you could do it so well", she replied.

David shook his head. He didn't know what Tamara was going

on about. He had been watching the sun set, and hadn't said a word.

He concentrated for a moment... it seemed like there was

something... He could barely remember thinking about... well to hell with it. It didn't matter He could tell by Tam's voice that she was needle-red into the Pissed Off Zone, and all it would take would be one misspoken word, and all the things they had done today would be ruined. He wasn't going to have that, not if he could help it. With a smile, he said, "You got it, babe. The man of a thousand voices, that's me."

She smiled. "Just don't jerk like that. I thought you were having a seizure, or something.

David smiled reassuringly. "You got it, pretty lady. No more doing the Chicken Dance for this trip. Now, how about head back to Pitlochry and see if I can wine you, dine you, and…

Tamara's hand clapped over David's mouth. With a grin, she said, "Don't even think about finishing that statement, Mr. Big-Shot Assistant County Attorney. Not unless you want to see just how hard Scottish floors can be, that is."

They walked back to the car in the gloaming and drove back into town. Dinner was excellent, and the dessert to die for, but all David wanted to talk about was their trip to Culloden the next day. Each time she tried to gently lead him off onto a different subject, he would invariably return to Culloden. It seemed to be the only thing he

seemed to want to talk about.

Three

The next morning dawned clear and cool. David was up nearly an hour before Tamara, which was weird, given the fact that back home she was the one that always had to yell at the lump of blankets that was her husband at least three times before he would get up in the morning. She sat up, shaking her sleep-muddled head and blinking owlishly at the clock on the nightstand as David raced from room to room, gathering their things. He stopped long enough to give her a quick kiss on top of the head and said, "Come on, Tam, we've got to get a move on. It's about seventy miles to Culloden, and the day's not getting any younger!" Tamara stared stupidly after him for a moment, and then finally asked in a sleep-hoarsened throat, "Who the hell are you, and what did you do with my husband?" David just grinned and shot past her again. Finally, she managed to rouse herself enough to swing her legs out and onto the floor. She staggered off to the bathroom, wondering what in the hell had gotten into her husband this morning.

They drove north, and by eleven-thirty that morning they were nearing the battlefield. Tamara reached into her purse and shook out three Tylenol tablets, which chased with a sip of coffee from their thermos. David was acting decidedly weird, she had decided. He was like a little boy on Christmas. He was also driving way to fast to suit her, since they still weren't properly used to rules of the road in this country. During the drive, he had prattled on ceaselessly about Culloden, its history, the battle, the aftermath, and anything else he could think of.

By the time we get there, she thought wryly, *there won't be any need to see the damn place.* She had always known of David's affinity for all things Scottish, he had married her in a kilt, for Christ's sake, but she didn't know he was also such a historian on the subject. His eyes alight, he talked excitedly about the battle that had taken place between the Governmental forces of the Duke of Cumberland and the Highlanders that had answered the call to arms from their clan chieftains to rally for

Prince Charles, otherwise known as Bonnie Prince Charlie, the Young Pretender.

The name Cumberland had struck a nerve in Tamara, and she turned her head to look at David while he spoke about him. She had finally gotten around to thinking that yesterday's little episode on the grounds of Castle Blair had been a joke, albeit a poor one, and now here he was talking about this Cumberland again. He gave no sign that he noticed her blank stare, but continued to spout facts and figures about the battle like some sort of pre-recorded automaton.

As it had last night, any attempt on her part to divert the conversation was met with a solid wall of indifference. He would seem to listen to her talking about the magnificent scenery around them for a few moments, and then return to the thread of his narrative. After several attempts, Tamara just sat back and looked out the window; making noncommittal grunts at what she thought were appropriate intervals.

For his part, David wasn't sure why he felt the way he did. He hadn't been this excited since the birth of his children, and to tell the truth, not even then. There was one thing that bothered him, though. He had been interested in Scottish history for many years, but he had never been a fanatic about it. He knew about the battle of Culloden, but his knowledge on the subject wasn't that vast. He knew about the battles of Falkirk and Stirling Bridge, and the grand rout of the English Forces on June 24, 1314 by Robert the Bruce at the Battle of Bannockburn, as well. He knew a little about each, but that was all. That being the case, where was all this information coming from? How did he know that the Battle of Bannockburn was called "Blàr Allt a' Bhonnaich" in Scottish Gaelic? He didn't speak but the odd word here and there. But it was the Battle of Culloden, *or "Blàr Chùil Lodair"*, he thought wryly, that his mind kept returning to. And why in the hell was he actually putting faces to the names he was talking about? He heard himself saying, "During the initial charge, a man named Hamish MacGregor took no less three musket balls to the body, two of which passed cleanly through his upper chest. He continued to charge, and after a hundred yards through icy water up to his ankles, put the blade of his basket hilt straight through the heart of one of Cumberland's men before he realized he'd been wounded at all." What David didn't, couldn't say was that Hamish MacGregor was six feet, four inches tall, had a full beard that fell to his chest, and was the youngest son of Ian

MacGregor. He further couldn't tell her that the man was prone to bouts of extreme flatulence, earning him the nickname "Windy MacGregor". David couldn't tell Tamara this because he no idea how in the hell he knew it himself. Somehow, he did know it, he could see the man's face in his mind like he was looking him eye-to-eye. David could have even described the small rill of scar tissue that meandered down MacGregor's cheek, disappearing into his full beard. Shaking his head, David went on to describe where and how the Governmental Dragoons were set up.

Four

They arrived at Culloden at noon and parked their car in the visitor's center lot. Tamara got out of the car slowly, stretching her ride-cramped legs. David was out of the car and halfway across the lot before she realized he wasn't standing by her. She gave an exasperated grunt and took off after him.

"Hey, dear heart, you want to wait a minute? I've heard about this damn place for the last four hours, and I would kind of like to see it with you, if you don't mind."

David stopped and turned to face her. Even from the distance between them, she could see his face contort, his brows lowering. He gave her a curt, one-handed "come on, then" gesture and turned back towards the large stone monument he had been staring at. She finally drew even with him and they walked on, although she almost had to jog to keep up with him. *What the hell is wrong with him?*

she wondered. They approached the stone, and she could see what was written there. The words were carved by hand, and looked old.

"The Battle of Culloden", she read out loud, "was fought on this moor 16th April 1746. The graves of the gallant Highlanders who fought for Scotland and Prince Charlie are marked by the names of their Clans." She turned to David. "April 16th is today, David. Today marks the two hundred and fifty-sixth anniversary of the battle. You forgot that little bit of trivia on the ride up here, sweetheart." She smiled at him, meaning to take some of the sting out of her remark, but the smile froze on her face as she saw him clearly. He was very pale, and his eye had taken on the blank look from the previous evening. He was muttering to himself almost inaudibly.

"Yes, today…have to hurry…almost time… just over that rise… quickly…"

With that, he spun on his heel and charged toward to battlefield, not sparing a glance at his wife. She walked as fast as she could behind him, a leaden ball of fear in her stomach, the coppery taste of panic in her throat. *To hell with all this,* she thought, *Battlefield be damned, we're going straight back to the hotel and then straight back home to the*

good ol' U.S. of A., the land where husbands don't turn into schizoids overnight.
She thought a second, and then amended *Well,* my *husband doesn't,*
anyway. She was on the verge of telling David this out loud when she
topped the small rise and got her first view of the battlefield itself. It
was the most desolate place she had ever seen in her life. There had
been nothing like it in all the things they had seen so far. The moor was
covered with yellow-orange grass, and there were pools of murky,
stagnant water here and there.

The whole place gave off an unmistakable sense of
desperation and suffering. She felt a chill run through her that had
nothing to do with the damp, cold Scottish wind, and she shuddered
uncontrollably. *Okay,* she thought, suddenly furious at her husband for
bringing her to such an awful place, *that's it. Fuck this place. I'm going back
to the car. David can play Boy Detective all he wants, but I'm not going one step
closer to that place, and that's it.*

She opened her mouth to yell at David's still-retreating
back when she was roughly shoved aside, causing her to give out an
indignant squawk. A huge man in a kilt strode by her. He was heavily
bearded and wore the period clothing she had seen in the paintings of

the Jacobite rebellion; however, this man looked like he hadn't eaten in days. His clothes were muddy and torn, and to Tamara's shock, he wore no shoes. His long legs flipped the hem of his kilt back and forth as he passed her by. He was carrying a musket over one shoulder, and had a flint-lock pistol shoved through his wide leather belt. On his hip was a large sword with a very ornate hilt. *Basket hilt broadsword*, she thought, *that's what David said those were.* In his left hand was a large circular shield of leather-covered wood decorated by studs of brass in intricate patterns. *Targe*, her mind reported. David had spent almost an hour describing just the weaponry involved in the battle, and she knew that the man passing her was in full Highland gear. Although, for a man of that time to have access to musket, pistol, sword, and shield, he would have had to been affluent, or come from a wealthy family. So where the hell were his shoes? *What the hell*, she thought, *maybe he's some sort of re-enactor.* If so, they certainly took reenactments seriously here. The man positively reeked of old sweat and God alone knew what else. She was all for keeping up with the history of one's homeland, but shoving tourist out of the way was not acceptable behavior, no matter how deep into his role the man was. Getting a grip on her temper, she said, "Hey! Why don't you look where you're...go...ing...." Her voice died in her throat. She gave out a breathless cry and slid to the ground.

The man in Highland gear had stopped at her voice, and had turned to face her. His face was unremarkable, maybe a little rough, but it wasn't his face that had caused Tamara's legs to fold under her like a card table. It was the man's eyes that had elicited that reaction. They were black. Not the deep, dark brown that most people call black, but coal mine black. And not just the pupils, either. All of his eyes were black, no cornea, no iris, just this oily black that glistened in the weak sunlight. He looked down at her for a moment and then growled at her.

"Suren' you need be off tha field the noo, lass. 'Tis not a place for a woman to be this day. Yer man will come tae hame this eve, or he won't. Nothin' that can be done, lassie. Now, get ye back wi' yer kin an' hold tae yer faith. We'll give these Sassenachs a fair show, an' tha scum that ride wi' them, at that. Off wi' ye. I'm to the lines, else I'll suren' miss the festivities."

With that, the man turned and strode away. Tamara sat on the soggy ground, totally unsure of what to do for the first time in her life. She had just been told to fuck off, albeit politely, by a… a… well, something, at any rate, and her husband seems to have lost his mind. As she sat there, it began to dawn on her that there were a great many voices now, and the sound of many marching feet. She could smell gunpowder in the air and heard the whinny of a frightened horse off in the distance. She could empathize completely with the animal, because she was scared shitless.

Regaining her feet, she began to scream "David! *David!*" as she topped the small rise. Her scream tapered down to a hoarse wail as she took in what she was seeing. Where an empty, desolate moor had been only moments ago, there were now lines of ragged men in Highland garb. A man on horseback was yelling at the men to *"Form up! Damn your eyes, form it up, here!"* She looked down the field and saw compact lines of men in crimson uniforms, facing the Highlanders. Tamara was a grounded woman. She had never seen a ghost, but that didn't mean that they didn't exist. *All right, Tamara, let's get a grip here,* she thought, trying to hold the panic that wanted to well up from inside her and overflow, *You are standing on an Eighteenth Century battlefield, and are apparently about to watch the battle. Never mind the fact that it is impossible, it's happening. Right now. So, since there is about to be a great deal shooting here in a very short time, what are you going to do right this instant? We'll worry about*

impossibilities later on, when there's less danger of getting shot and killed.

"I'll tell you what I'm going to do", she said, "I'm

getting the fuck out of here, right now, post-haste. I love ya, Scotland,

but you can kiss my ass."

She looked frantically around for David and finally saw

him about a hundred yards away, talking to an older Scot in dress

clothes. She began walking purposefully toward him, dancing around

the knots of men that were hurrying towards the lines at the front. As

she neared David, she saw that he had taken off his leather bomber

jacket and thrown it to the ground and was putting on a ragged, yet

serviceable coat of the same pattern as the older Scot's. She didn't

register it at once, but when he began strapping on a large broad sword

and reaching for a musket, she lost it completely. She ran full-tilt and

collided with him. The impact caused him to drop the musket. With a

speed she didn't know he possessed, David bent at the knees and

neatly caught the musket still a foot off the ground.

He whipped around to face her. "Dammit, Tamara,

watch where you're going! These things won't fire if they get wet!"

At first she was so taken aback that she lost her voice. Her throat worked convulsively. Finally, her throat unlocked and she screamed directly into her husband's face.

"David, what in the *HELL ARE YOU DOING?!?*" We have to go! Can't you see what's going on here? Jesus!"

David looked at her for a moment, his eyes cloudy with thought. He closed them for a second, and then shook his head and opened his eyes again. They were full of sorrow and wonder, a combination Tamara had never seen before. His voice was tender.

"No, Tam. I can't go anywhere right now. I have to talk to Lord George Murray. The line is going to break; the Highland charge won't work here." At this point David turned his eyes towards a distant figure on horseback, far back from the lines. Disgust lined his voice when he continued. "The Clans all know that they can't win here, not like this, but that little Italian fop and his Irish yes-man don't." Here, his voice rose to a yell directed towards the distant horseman, who was busily giving orders left and right. *"Cum do theanga ablaich gun fheum! De do ghnothaich!"*

Tamara looked at her husband as if he had grown an extra head. "What the hell was that?"

David looked slightly abashed. "I, uh… I can sort of speak Gaelic now."

She nodded, as of this were the most natural thing in the world. "And how long have you been hiding this little light under your basket?" she said, her voice remarkably calm. "And what, pray tell, did you yell at him?"

Again David looked embarrassed. "Well, I told him to shut up, that he was an idiot, and to mind his own business, actually." He shook himself like a wet dog and got back to his main theme, "Look, Tam, these men are going to be slaughtered. Look at that field. Could you run the length of it in ankle-deep water faster than the Sassenachs could reload? But I know what happens, Tam! I can tell them and end the slaughter before it starts! I've just got to get to Lord Murray and explain. We can win this time, Tam!" His eyes were ablaze with excitement,

Tamara Roberts had never been so angry in her entire life. All the little things she had grown to hate about her husband suddenly burst forth like water from a broken dyke. Her voice cut cleanly through the voices on the field, even the Government troops stopping for a second to hear.

"We can win? *WE* can win? *WE???* You are a lawyer from Virginia, you dumb bastard!!! There is no '*we*' here! There is an '*Us*' and there is a '*Them*', and in case you hadn't noticed, the 'Them' in this equation have been DEAD FOR ALMOST THREE HUNDRED FUCKING YEARS!!!"

David took an involuntary step backwards. From various places on the field, laughter could be heard, even from the Government troops. "Gie 'im what for, lassie!", someone yelled, "Dinna be takin' aught from 'im!"

David seemed to get his bearings. He walked to her and took her by the arms. He looked into her eyes. What she saw there frightened her badly. He meant to do it. Regardless of anything else, he meant to do it. He smiled at her, trying to lighten the impact of what he was saying.

"Tam, there will be almost fifteen hundred Highlanders killed right here, in this spot, in less than an hour. And they will be the lucky ones. After the battle, the Duke of Cumberland orders every wounded man left alive on the field killed. And it doesn't stop there. The families of these men, and even those that didn't take the Prince's side are put out of hearth and home, their livestock either killed or stolen, the men of their houses taken out and shot, even if they had been nowhere near the battle. After this battle, the Sassenachs, I mean the *English*, pass laws forbidding kilts, bagpipes…anything Scottish. It is the beginning of the end of the Clans. Soon after this, there will come a time of horror on the Scottish people that they haven't seen since King Edward I" David looked away into the middle distance for a moment, and then looked back into her eyes. "I can change that. That's why I'm here, now. I can change it, and I'm *going to do it*!"

Before she knew what was happening, David gave her a solid kiss on the mouth and then said something in Gaelic to the two Highlanders that seemed to have appeared out of nowhere behind her. They took her gently, yet with determination, and began to pull her off the field. She struggled violently, but it was like attacking two oak trees. She began screaming.

"David! David, no! NO!!! Please, David, please come with me! Let go of me, you fucking bastards!!! David! *PLEEEEEASE!!!*"

Her last vision of her husband was of David raising his hands to his mouth and blowing her kisses from both closed fists, like he had when they had dated and had first gotten married. As she was dragged away, she heard him say, "*Tha gael agam ort, mo chridhe!*" And then he was gone. She felt herself go limp in the hands of the Highlanders. She felt them lay her gently to the ground and heard their footsteps as they moved away. Her stomach gave a flip and a wave of vertigo hit her. *I'll be damned,* she thought, *I'm fainting. That's a first.*

The sound of marching men followed her into the blackness.

Five

She came to the surface slowly, like a bubble in a jar of oil. Someone was shaking her. *It's David*, she thought. *It's time to get up and go to Culloden. Culloden.* That brought her up fast and she sat up. She looked around groggily A young policeman was kneeling before her, gently shaking her. With a look of relief, he smiled at her.

"There we are, mum", he said. "Thought we'd lost you for a wee bit there."

Tamara looked around and realized that she was sitting on the asphalt of the parking lot. She stood shakily to her feet, helped by the policeman. She looked around for David, thinking that if he couldn't do any better than to make sure his unconscious wife was all right before going to look at a damned battlefield, then she had a thing or two to say to him.

There were many people walking about the visitor's center and along the trails of the battlefield, but Tamara couldn't locate David among them. Still leaning on the policeman, she asked, "Have you by any chance seen a man, American, about five foot eight, sandy hair with some grey in it?

The policeman shook his head, but smiled and said, "I'm sure he's about, mum. Today is always chaotic, to be sure. Seems like half the country is here."

Tamara shook her head. "Really? I must have hit my head or something when I fell, because when we got here at noon, there wasn't a soul in sight. How long have I been laying there?"

The policeman was now looking at her with concern in his eyes. "Are you sure you don't need an ambulance, mum?"

Tamara shook her head. "No, I'm fine. I just need to find David. Maybe he's over at the monument…"

Her voice trailed off as she stood before the stone monolith. She would have fallen if not for the policeman at her side to catch her. She looked at the monument. It looked the same, but now it read, "The Battle of Culloden was fought on this moor 16th April 1746. Here was won the Freedom of Scotland, and the Restoration of her Rightful King, James IV, and his son Prince Charles Edward Stuart."

Tamara looked at the tribute a long time and then smiled. "You did it, you crazy son of a bitch. You actually did it."

The policeman smiled uncertainly at her. "What was that, love?"

Tamara shook her head. "Nothing. I just need to go look for my husband. Wait a second, do you happen to know any Gaelic?"

The policeman laughed. "Well, to be certain I do, mum. It's the official language of Scotland, ye know. English is the second language. Of course, we only use English whenever you Yanks come over, or one of the Sassenachs gets off their high horse and pays us a visit. Why?"

She was confused for a minute, thinking that should be the other way around, but then let it go. "I was wondering if you knew what *'Tha gael agam ort, mo chridhe'* means."

The policeman smiled again. "It means 'I love you, my heart'. It's a way of saying that a person is the very heart and soul of you."

Tamara smiled. "I'll have to remember that. Thank you so very much for all your help. I'm going to find my husband now."

The policeman tipped his hat to her and said, "Well, if you're sure you're all right, I'll be on me way. Good day to you, mum." He started off across the parking lot.

Tamara looked at the stone monument once more, amazed at the pride she felt well up inside her. He had done it. A lawyer from Virginia had changed the course of history. She started away, thinking of all the things she wanted to say to him, when a smaller stone marker caught her eye. It sat just off to the left of the big monument, and was an old Celtic cross on a stone base, the whole of it standing about four feet high. Curious, she read the inscription.

David Roberts, beloved of Tamara, it read, fell this 16th April 1746 in defense of Scotland. "But for him, all would have been lost."- Lord George Murray.

The damp, chill Scottish wind blew across the moor, rustling through the Highland rose, sweeping through the heather, its sound unable to stifle the sound of a woman that stood weeping at the grave of her husband, her shoulders shaking with silent grief.

Modern Psychiatry

The tinted windows of the doctor's office transformed the sunny September day into a tropical storm in waiting. Kyle leaned across the table in the corner of the waiting room and picked up an issue of 'People' magazine that was two months out of date. With an inward sigh, he began scanning the articles about celebrities in whom he had no interest whatsoever.

There were four other occupants in the waiting room. An elderly lady with garish make up and steel-blue haired, a thirty-something man in an expensive business suit. A young married couple, he with bright, intelligent eyes, she drooling and staring vacantly into space. Kyle named them in his mind, a game from childhood. The old lady was Mary Kay. The suit was Captain Ulcer. The man was the Professor, his wife Slobberjaws. Kyle grinned as he stared through a picture of J. Lo and Ben Affleck cavorting on an unnamed beach. Kyle knew their real names, of course. He knew everything about them. Mary Kay was Mrs. Josepha Kurtz. She was here to see Dr. Lydon about a compulsive gambling habit. Captain Ulcer was Donald Brookman. His visit was court ordered. The Louisiana Bar Association had agreed to allow him to continue practicing law on the condition

that he enroll in anger management therapy. One doesn't punch a

fellow attorney in the throat simply because one disagrees with said

attorney's objection to a line of questioning. Not in Louisiana, anyway.

The Professor and Slobberjaws were Mr. and Mrs. Ferrell and Nancy

Kallen. Ferrell was in charge of park design for the Louisiana State

Park Service, and Nancy had been a registered nurse until the

kidnapping and subsequent murder of their three year old son, Seth, a

year earlier. Since then, Nancy had remained catatonic. The Kallens

were at Dr. Lydon not for Nancy, but for Ferrell. He was finding the

strain of a lost child, a zombified wife, and a demanding job slowly

becoming more than he could bear. Kyle would have felt bad for the

Kallens, if he were capable of such a thing.

Kyle himself was there for his weekly visit with Dr. Lydon, or

as Kyle inwardly called him, "Pencil-Dick". The first two months had

been kind of fun, watching Pencil-Dick fumble about like a child

searching for a night light. Listening to his pompous proclamations

about Kyle's "inability to emotionally bond", had actually evoked a

silent gust of laughter from Kyle. The novelty had begun to wear out,

and now Kyle tired of this sport. He wondered if the time had not, perhaps, come to pull a fade and move on. He found this prospect

satisfying, and, as with all decisions in his life, he never questioned it at

all. *What the fuck,* Kyle thought, *I'll leave today.*

He sat thumbing through his tattered magazine and patiently

waited for his name to be called. Mary Kay was called first, her eyes

shifting back and forth, back and forth. She muttered under her breath

as she shuffled past the secretary into the doctor's office. Kyle stared

bemusedly after her. All at once, the day's possibility overwhelmed him

and he laughed out loud, a high, crystal sound. Captain Ulcer let fly a

surprised grunt and fixed Kyle with a baleful glare. The Professor

merely gave Kyle a gentle smile and turned back to his wife. With slow

movements of his hand, he wiped her spittle-covered chin. *Yes,* Kyle

thought, *the Professor was good people...whatever that means.* Kyle looked back

out of the window and watched the late summer bugs sluggishly cut

their geometric patterns in the falsely darkened sky.

Just over forty-five minutes later, Mary Kay walked out into the

waiting room, her nervous eyes still dancing. She was speaking

earnestly to Pencil-Dick. He was nodding and giving his patented

"Comforting Smile".

As he nodded, he steered Mary Kay towards the secretary's desk, undoubtedly to make another appointment. He noticed Kyle and gave a small wave, then turned and went back into his office. Kyle stood, knowing that he was about to be called back into the inner sanctum. *Ride me hard, Commander Freud*, he thought with a smile. *All aboard the Starship Id.*

He took a few steps toward the door, then paused and turned back to face the waiting room. He cleared his throat and said, "Could I have everyone's attention for a moment? Thank you." All eyes turned expectantly towards him. With a sunny grin, he said, "Now, folks, this won't hurt one bit, and I appreciate your time." Kyle's eyes flashed with brilliant white light, twin supernovas in miniscule. As one, the occupants of Dr. Lydon's waiting room convulsed and slithered to the floor, blood pouring from their eyes, ears, mouths, and noses. Kyle glanced around, admiring his handiwork. To his surprise, Slobberjaws was struggling to sit up. He stared at her for a moment, his head cocked at a slight angle. She tried to speak, but it came out garbled. With obvious effort, she turned, spat out a large amount of bright red blood, and tried again.

"...thank...you..."

Kyle's smile burst forth, sunlight through the clouds. "Hey, no problem!" he said. "Just doing my part for the war effort and all!" Slobberjaws slid slowly back, her eyes black with hemorrhaged blood. Kyle once again surveyed the scene before him. God-Damn, but it was nice to be young and to truly enjoy one's work, he thought. With that same sunny grin, he turned to Pencil-Dick's office. This was going to prove to be an enlightening bit of psychiatry. Kyle was positive they never covered this material in Pencil-Dick's alma mater. And beyond that, the promise of a world, waiting. Kyle turned and opened the door.

Road to Bifrost

The hall lay silent, its hearth filled with frozen logs of a long ago fire. Ice-darkened windows creaked in the ceaseless wind. A huge table ran the length of the hall, and upon it sat the remains of a meal. Wooden cups, mead frozen to a hard crust within them, lay interspersed among the plates of food. Half-gnawed bones and rinds of dark bread lay about, giving the indication of a meal interrupted. The hall itself was long and dark, its vaulted ceilings reaching some forty feet high. The floor was of cobbled stone. The fireplace was massive, large enough to roast even the largest of beasts whole. Around the table, at intervals of five feet, sat high-backed chairs, each made of oak and bone. On the wall behind each chair hung weapons of different types; a sword behind one, an axe behind another. Round wooden shields, each emblazoned with a different design painted upon its surface, hung by straps under the weapons. Covering all was a thick layer of frost.

At the end of the table was the largest chair of all. Perched atop it were two ravens, their glossy feathers dulled with frost. They appeared to be frozen as solid as the chair upon which they sat. Beside the chair was a pedestal holding and ice-encrusted crystal globe. The globe was dark, save for tiny flecks of light that bounced around its interior like miniature meteors.

Suddenly, these lights began to grow in intensity and their bouncing became more agitated. The globe issued a loud cracking, and ice began to fall away in large chunks to smash to the floor like glass. Within moments, the globe was free of its icy covering and gave off a bright, steady glow that lit the hall.

The globe gave off no warmth at all, and yet the ravens soon began quivering, frost sliding off their feathers like a soft snow. After several moments, the ravens shook themselves and gave twin cries. They took wing and flew to the pedestal. They perched there and spent several minutes peering into the depths of the globe. They sat this way a long while, their bright eyes watching closely, their heads cocking from side to side. Finally, with another cry, they took off and flew down the passageway at the end of the hall. They passed several iron-banded wooden doors on either side of the passageway until they came to a door at the far end. They landed on the floor and hopped up to the door. They seemed to carry on a brief, silent conversation with each other until finally, one hopped forward and rapped upon the door, its beak giving a sharp crack against the frozen wood.

The door creaked open, its rust-clotted hinges screaming in protest. The ravens hopped into the room. It was Spartan, the only furnishings a bed and a chair nearby next to a fireplace. The ravens flew to the chair and gave their odd, over-lapping cries. There was no immediate response. The ravens shared a look that was unmistakably irritated, and turned to the fireplace. They cried out again, this time their voices rising and lowering in a warble. The dead logs burst into flame. From the bed there issued a deep grumble. The ravens flew to the bedposts and perched there. After another moment, one of them bobbed its head and rapped at the figure lying on the bed.

With another grumble, the fur was flung back and a massive figure swung its legs out of bed. Sitting in the jumble of fur blankets was an old man. His hair fell to his waist, and his beard lay in a platted knot down his chest. Both were snow-white. A leather patch covered his right eye, and a ribbon of twisted scar tissue snaked from under it down his cheek. He was broad shouldered and heavily muscled, and he moved with an agility that belied his age.

He stood stretching his large frame, his joints popping like pine knots in a fire. He cast a sour look at the ravens. Undaunted, they flew to him and landed on his shoulders. The old man grinned ruefully and scratched them on their heads. He walked over to the chair and picked up a rough leather jerkin from it. As he pulled it over his head, the ravens took wing and flew across the room to land near the door. The old man flapped his hand at them, *go on, then,* as he began pulling on leather breeches and knee-high boots.

He followed them down the darkened passageway into the main hall. His breath formed crystals with each exhalation from his mighty lungs. He rubbed his gnarled hands together and gave the ravens a reproachful look. They seemed to grin back at him, and then gave their odd, two-toned warble again. A fire burst forth from the massive hearth, and the old logs began to burn like dry tinder. The old man stood before the fire a few moments, warming himself. Then he walked to the weapons that hung behind the largest chair at the end of the table. With slow deliberation, he drew on his armor and picked up a many-notched axe and a gigantic spear. He turned to the ravens, which were perched on the pedestal again, peering into the globe. He sat down beside the globe and shooed them away. With indignant cries, they flew to the table and began to forage through the left-over food upon it.

The old man grunted in amusement and then looked into the globe. He passed a hand over it and its glow brightened to the point that he was forced to squint to look into it. He passed his hand over it again, and the glow subsided. In its place came a milky fog within the globe. The mist began to form rudimentary shapes, and after a few moments, he could make out the forms of many men, all in rows. He was almost able to see them clearly when his attention was jerked away from the globe. From far away there came a long howl. It grew in intensity until the frosted windows shook within their frames.

The old man leapt to his feet, his hand tightening on the shaft of his spear. The howl faded into silence. The old man stood waiting, but the howl was not repeated. With a dark look, the old man returned to the globe. The shapes had lost definition, returning to mist. He passed his hand again, and they began to reform. From the mist, he could now see vast armies, each man dressed identically. The old man was surprised to see that they wore no armor, save a metal helmet. Their chests and legs were exposed, covered only in cloth, no mail nor plating visible. The old man chuckled. He could go through these men like a scythe if he wished. He looked closer, and with a start, realized that the warriors carried neither sword nor axe, shield nor spear. They carried nothing but a small knife on their sides in a leather sheath. Each man carried what appeared to be small iron pole set in a wooden handle. As far as the old man could tell, these small spears had no points upon them.

The old man shook his head, unsure how these men could be effective in battle. He looked closely at them, trying to understand what he was seeing. His eyes trailed across the ranks of men, and suddenly he gasped. On each man's arm was a red band, and upon that was the svashtika, the emblem he himself bore upon his shield. He looked at his shield and back to the emblem on the men's sleeves. Something was amiss. After a few moments, he realized that the emblem was backward on the men, its four points leaning to the right, instead of to the left as proper. Still, he thought, this must be a sign of sorts.

As he watched, the armies marched across a field towards another army of men on horseback. He watched with interest to see how the helmeted me would defend themselves against the horsemen.

Suddenly, great gouts of flame burst into the air, and the horsemen were flung to the ground, torn apart. The old man looked back to the marching soldiers and gave another gasp. Rolling among them were huge metal beasts with a single long arm. From this arm burst smoke and fire. The old man gave a fierce cry. These warriors had trapped the fire-worms in these metal cases, and were using them to fight the battle. True warriors they must be, he thought, to have managed to capture so many dragons.

The old man watched with renewed interest and soon noted that the marching soldiers were pointing their wood and metal spears at the remaining horsemen. Smaller flames licked the end of these and the horsemen continued to fall. The old man began to understand that these small spears gave forth barbs that flew faster than a man could see, and impaled the enemy. The old man bashed his leg with a massive fist in his excitement. These were warriors of true cunning. Even his berserkers would have a difficult time taking down these men.

He searched the globe further, trying to locate the chieftain of these warriors among them. He was disappointed to find that the leader was not among the men on the field. With a gesture, he instructed the globe to find this man. The mist swirled and began to

take shape again. The view cleared and showed a vast gathering of

people, more people than the old man had ever seen on one place

before. Huge banners hung all around, each brilliant red and sporting

the backwards svashtika. On a raised podium in front of the crown

stood the man who appeared to be the leader. The old man looked

dubiously at him. The man at the podium was small in stature, and

even had no proper beard. The smallest of the old man's warriors

would have no problem defeating this one, he thought. He strained

hard and was able to hear what the man was saying. The voice issuing

from the globe was tinny, as if spoken inside a metal drum. The old

man could almost understand what was being said, but not quite. It was

if someone was speaking his language with an odd accent, and adding

nonsense words. He listen a short while longer and then shook his

head. No, he could not fathom what was being said, but the funny little

man was very vehement about whatever it he was saying. The vast

crowd swayed in time with him, and it was obvious he held them in

thrall.

As difficult as it was to believe, this strange little man was the

leader of the armies the old man had seen. He sat back in his chair, his face set in deep concentration. Suddenly, the howl reverberated throughout the hall once again. It was closer now, more urgent. The old man barely noticed, his single blue eye staring off into the distance. So, he thought. It was time. He would awaken the others, for they must prepare for the coming battle. He heaved himself upright, and turned to go back down the hall. He gave once final glance at the globe, and stopped short.

The scene had changed. The soldiers he had seen earlier, or more just like them, were now herding people into long, box-like carriages. Men, women, and children, the old and young alike, were crowded into these boxes. The globe misted again and when it cleared, these same people were being driven off the carriages and through large iron gates. The gates had something written upon them, but it was not in Runic, so the old man could not make it out. Just inside the gates, the men were separated from the women and children, and then sent into vast buildings, given tattered uniforms, and sent out to work the fields.

The women and children, as well as the old and infirm, were sent into similar buildings, where they were stripped naked and shoved rudely into large rooms with a single door. The old man gave a growl as he realized that these people were all being killed in some strange way. Naked and shivering, they were packed into the rooms so tightly they could not move. Soon, some magic smoke came down from the ceiling and killed them where they stood, screaming in pain and fear.

After what seemed like hours, the dead were carted away to massive furnaces to be burned, their clothing and treasure looted by the soldiers. The old man, shaking with rage, began pacing back and forth in front of the hearth. *This cannot be,* he thought. These were not warriors, regardless of how well the preformed in battle! Yes, he had seen innocents slain, had done so himself, but only if they were in the way of the battle. He did not go looking for unarmed peasants to kill, nor did any man that wished to ride the war-boat with him. He stopped pacing and stood looking into the fire. With a sudden nod, he went back to the globe.

The horrid scenes of slaughter were gone, the mist having re-formed. The old man sent for the leader of the armies to be found again. The mist cleared, and the little mustached man was lying asleep in his richly upholstered bed. The old man stared at the globe intensely for a moment. Soon, the little man began twitching in his sleep. Sweat popped out all over his body, and he began to cry out in terror. Nightmares gripped him. The old man bore down with all his considerable will, and felt the small man's mind snap.

With a satisfied nod, the old man stood, passing a hand over the globe. It immediately fell dark. Now, the man that was leading the vast armies would no longer be able to perform correctly. The old man had driven him mad. Not that it had taken much to do so, the old man thought, he was near madness to begin with. The armies of the madman would fail, in time.

From outside the hall, the howl from earlier rose again, only this time it was far away and dim. The old man grinned grimly. Fenrir would have to wait longer yet, thought the old man. He slowly took off his armor and replaced it behind his chair. The ravens flew over to him and received their accustomed pats on the head. They then flew back to their places on the chair and settled in, the frost already beginning to form on their feathers.

The old man walked back down the hall towards his room.

Well, thought Odin, *at least I figured out what was going on before waking the others.*

Thor was such a grouch when he first woke up.

Stupperware

On Tuesday, May 24th, 951 A.D., at precisely twelve noon Greenwich Mean Time, Stupper IV,

a small, oxygen-rich planet approximately ninety-six million light years from Earth became enlightened. For millennia, the inhabitants of Stupper IV had struggled to reach said enlightenment. Through war, famine, draught, disease, and pestilence, the Stupps, as they referred to themselves, slowly gained the knowledge necessary to create a Utopian society. Boundaries disappeared, and racially different Stupps embraced one another as brothers. In this atmosphere of harmony, science made quantum leaps forward. Sickness became a thing of myth, war, a story to tell around campfires to scare children.

For two thousand, five hundred years, the Stupps advanced in peace and harmony. They became the model set for all other planets in the system to follow. Word of the beauty and grace of this perfect society spread into surrounding systems, and beings of all types made pilgrimages to Stupper IV to view for themselves this marvel.

Then, in the Earth year 1998, a strange illness overcame the Stupps. The whole society fell stricken, avoiding the bright light of their sunlit fields, lying about on couches made of synthetic animal fur. (The use of animal pelts had been deemed barbaric thousands of years earlier. This was all well and good, except the Stupps hadn't come up with an alternative method of covering themselves at that time. Millions of Stupps quietly froze to death that winter, while the native fur-bearing fauna looked on with open amusement.)

For many seasonal cycles, the inhabitants of Stupper IV suffered this strange new illness. The symptoms:

1.)   A complete lack of desire to move any more than was necessary to make occasional trips to the bathroom or the refrigerator,

2.) A swelling of the abdomen, coupled with a bulging of the posterior regions,

3) A sickly pallor, red-rimmed and bloodshot eyes, and,

4) An out-right hatred of anything even vaguely having to do with manual labor.

The best minds of Stupper IV worked diligently to find a cure, or rather, would have if they had deigned to work at all. For several years this disease continued, unabated, until it seemed that the Stupps were doomed to slow, lazy extinction.

Just as all hope faltered, a young Stupp by the name of Jerius Malikain made a startling discovery. One afternoon he was lying on his synthetic fur couch when he was struck with a sudden urge for a cold glass of Verlak, the Stuppian equivalent of Coors Light. He gazed longingly at the refrigerator. He weighed his desire for the Verlak over the immense effort the fourteen steps to the refrigerator would take, and decided that yes, dammit, it was worth it. With a heavy sigh, he heaved his bulk off the couch and began his trek to the fridge. An hour and a half later, a very winded Jerius Malikain stood at the end of his quest. With sweat pouring off his face in torrents, he smiled and, with one final burst of energy, opened the refrigerator door. The triumphant smile curdled on his face, and his eyes, only seconds before full of serene happiness, blazed forth with an unbridled rage. For there, with the cold blue light of the refrigerator bringing the world into hellish contrast, stood an empty shelf where once his Verlak had stood.

Jerius Malikain stood, jaw agape for several long moments. A vein rose upon his forehead, grotesquely throbbing with each beat of his enraged heart. That is to say, it throbbed no less than three times a minute. May not sound like much to you, but brother, for a Stupp, that's some kind of pissed. His eyes bulged out onto their stalks until the left one was dragging the floor and the right one was almost brushing the ceiling. A half-articulated scream of fear, surprise, and rage danced just behind his lips, making them jump about in all sorts of odd contortions.

His mind raced feverishly, trying to take in all this data and turn it into something that made some modicum of sense. Being of a scientific race, the Stupp began to go through a series of short experiments. He closed the refrigerator door, then opened it again. No Verlak. He shut it half way, then closed one eye and reopened it. No Verlak. He stood on his head, closed both eyes, and then shut the door on his lips. When he reopened it, there was still no Verlak to be found, but his lips were decidedly more pronounced. (This began a fad that lasted well into the next millennia. Upon human contact with the Stuppian race, it was called the Jagger Effect. While interesting, this has nothing to do with the current chronicle, and as such, shall be removed from this story. Sorry about that.)

Jerius Malikain was stymied. He was perplexed. He was confused to the *n*th. He was, in a word, fucked. He began to settle in for what would undoubtedly be several hours of soft weeping when a thought bubble rose to the surface of his mind, and with a sound like a mouse farting, burst.

His roommate, Kindeian Harwinder, was sitting on a couch in the living room. Had been sitting there for months. Jerius should know, since he sat not four feet away on his couch the whole time. For months, neither had moved...except for once. Jerius had a hazy recollection of Kindeian mumbling something about needing to go to the bathroom a few weeks ago. Jerius had grunted noncommittally and gone back to watching a show on television about the mating habits of the Seven-Cocked Grendolen of Feriun III. As he now thought back to that time, he realized that Kindeian had been gone for four days, instead of the customary three days it took to get to the bathroom and back. With a stab of suspicion, Jerius yelled into the living room.

"Kindeian, did you by any chance drink my Verlak?"

Almost two hours later, Kindeian replied, "Yeah, I got thirsty on my way back from the bathroom."

What happened next became known to the Stuppian race as "The Really Big Event". In a flash, Jerius Malikain was towering over Kindeian Harwinder, pummeling him with big, soft cushions from the couch. This was the first time in years that a Stupp had moved at anything over 0.0001 miles per hour.

It was such a horrifying break from the norm of Stuppian feuding (which involved taunts hurled back and forth at each other over the space of weeks), that poor Kindeian Harwinder's genitalia exploded in self-defense.

In days, word that a Stuppian had showed the ability to move rapidly was all over Stupper IV. Scientists began formulating hypotheses that perhaps the lethargy that had covered Stupper IV like a thick film was internally induced. This was a far reach from the original theory that a giant cloud of free-floating chloroform had come to roost over the planet's polar cap. After several weeks of heated discussion, the scientific community of Stupper IV gave this startling announcement (As quoted from 'StuppNerd Magazine, Issue 23'):

"After long and careful deliberation, and the weighing of all the facts, it is the conclusion of this panel that the long-running sickness, formerly known as "I-Feel-Like-Total-Shit-Today-And-I'm-Not-Moving-A-Fucking-Muscle-Even-If-I-Catch-Fire" disease, is, in fact caused by one thing... total boredom."

The article then went on to explain how it is possible to render solid gold from the fecal matter of a chipmunk, but that, while enlightening, isn't very relevant here. Soon, the whole planet was alight with new-found possibility. All they needed was something to keep their attention, something to keep the fire burning within their weary, fat-assed souls. But what? As mentioned earlier, Stupper IV had conquered all its problems. There was nothing to unite the people in motion. At a world-wide council, Jerius Malikain, now a world-wide hero of the Stuppish people, made this suggestion:

"Well, we could always re-invent class warfare."

The crowd went positively wild. Of course! Class warfare would keep the people going for years! The only problem was how to divide the populace into different classes, none too easy a task on a planet where everyone had exactly the same status. After much thought, they finally devised a method...

And that is how, on the twenty-ninth day of Bartoq, in the year of the Equine Quadruped Mammalian, the planet Stupper IV became known the galaxy-wide for hosting the largest ever Paper, Rock, Scissors game in recorded history.

Epilogue

For those of you that wished to know the eventual outcome of the Stuppian class warfare, I regret to inform you that there were no clear winners, nor losers. Not long after the institution of the system, and just, might I add, when the Stupps were really starting to cook, having just re-invented rocket-propelled grenades and put them to use, their planet suffered a cataclysmic event that doomed the whole race to extinction.

It seems, by all accounts, that Stupper IV was mostly destroyed when an Ursalian Space Cow wandered into the system, and as a result of grazing wild in the Fire Fields of the Andovver Nebula, burnt most of the system to a crisp with a horrendous bout of flatulence. While the tragedy weighed heavy in this narrator's mind, he is happy to report that he kept 'StuppNerd Magazine, Issue 23', and is running a ludicrous chipmunk farm on the outskirts of Seattle, Washington.

Hill 108

The boys of 2nd Platoon were tired. Dog tired, to be exact. Or, if you want to be perfectly blunt, we were dog *fucking* tired. We had finally made it to the summit of Hill 108, after eight continuous days of combat. Charlie had dug himself in deep this time. We had taken Hill 108 from him three times in the last eight months, and were getting pretty sick and tired of looking at it.

According to Daniels, the Air Force had blown two and a half feet off the top of the hill since the assault began this time. That was all well and good, if it wasn't for the fact that Charlie was dug in one whole hell of a lot deeper than two and a half feet.

Daniels wanted to be a pilot more than anything in the world. He had repeatedly volunteered for the Air Force, and had been repeatedly turned down. Physically, he was all right, but he was only a few I.Q. points away from an institutionally eligible retard. Which, of course, meant that the infantry wanted him. Know which end of the rifle is the dangerous one? Yes? Congratulations, son, you're in the Army now.

I sat on an uprooted tree, eating C-rations that had been canned right about the time Hitler was munching on a 9mm honeymoon sandwich. As I chewed on something unidentifiable, I looked around at the rest of 2nd Platoon. We were dispersed around the crest of the hill, some in half-demolished bunkers, and others lying full on the ground with their helmets over their faces. *So this is the modern army,* I thought. *Lovely.* We looked like a bunch of refugees from a concentration camp. If it wasn't for the napalm and burnt flesh, you could have smelled any one of us from fifty yards away. I myself was no prom queen. The bottom half of one of my B.D.U. legs had been ripped away during the last assault, so I cut the other one away, as well, and made myself some shorts. Sgt. Ferris cocked one eye over at me while I was performing this operation and grunted.

"Samuels, you're gonna wish like hell you had them legs tonight when a snake crawls up your pants and bites your pecker off."

The thought of a reptile gnawing on my genitalia didn't hold the terror it once might have. It's kind of hard to get worked up about something as stupid as a snake in 'Nam. I grinned back at Sgt. Ferris, my eyes disappearing like they always did when I smiled.

"Well, Sarge, it had better be a fuckin' python, or my tremendous Johnson will scare it the righteous fuck away."

Ferris shook his head, and lay back with his doo-rag covering his eyes.

"Y'all are 'bout spastic, Samuels. Y' momma have any young 'uns that lived?"

Ferris was the absolute stereotype of all Sergeants. He hailed from Shreveport, Louisiana, and was as big a redneck as you could ever meet. He chewed a nasty-smelling plug of tobacco, and professed to be able to "hit a fly in the ass from a hunnert yards out in a high wind". I could attest to his shooting skills. Once, during a monsoon, I had seen him shoot a V.C. sapper right through the top of the skull from about ninety yards away, with only the light of parachute flares to aid him. Ninety yards may not sound like much, but try it in a downpour so hard you can barely see the man next to you, and the wind howling and changing directions constantly. No seriously, try it sometime, see how well you do, although I suggest that unless it's war time, you use a paper target, or you'll wind up in prison.

Ferris was, like sergeants all over the world, the backbone of the unit. He was always there, ready to give a hand if it was needed, or to give a boot in the ass if he felt *that* was needed. He was built like a barn, square and blocky. There was something about him, this sense of forever. That's the best I can describe it. The only other thing I've ever gotten that feeling when I've looked at it was the Sphinx. It was on that kind of level. When you looked at Sgt. Ferris, you felt an invincibility coming from him, a feel of stone. It wasn't that he looked heroic or anything like that. He just gave off a vibe. It was like the rock outcropping I walked by on my way to school when I was a kid. It was always there, and you knew it always would be, comforting in its very substance. Of course, neither the rock outcrop nor the Sphinx was prone to amazingly long bouts of flatulence that sounded like a tuba.

Over to my left sat Cpl. Anthony Markum. He was studying his feet myopically. He was a regular bear about his feet. He swore up and down that his feet were going to rot off right from under him. We gave him such hell over that. Don't get me wrong, a week in the 'Nam, and your feet actually could rot off if you'd didn't watch out, but with a little care you'd make out all right. Markum didn't believe any of it. If we had to hump an overly-long distance, he'd gripe constantly that we needed to stop so he could change socks. Once, he had bitched so long and so loud that Sgt. Ferris threatened to dip both his feet in Water Buffalo shit if he didn't shut up. From the look on his face, you'd have thought that Ferris had just threatened to eat his grandmother with some fried rice and a bottle of Kirian beer. He shut up, though.

His fascination with his feet had earned him the nickname "Wiggles", due to the way he was constantly wiggling his toes as he studied them. This was later shortened to "Wiggs". We put up with his constant whining in no small part because of his gift with radios. He could take a field radio that had just been ripped apart by small arms fire, and in ten minutes, be calling in close air support. This was a very useful, and much appreciated, talent in 'Nam. He was currently digging at something between his toes with his bayonet.

"Hey, Wiggs", I called over to him, "You diggin' for fuckin' gold, or what?"

"There's some sort of black shit between my toes", he said in a nasal whine. "I think I need a medic."

I got up and chucked the remains of my C-Rat over the hill, and walked over. I leaned over and took a close look at his toes.

"Shit, Wiggs that *does* look bad."

His eyes widened. He glared back at his toes as if he was about to give them a good dressing down.

"I fuckin' knew it. I fuckin' *knew* it. I haven't been able to keep them clean for shit since we started this tits-up. What do you think it is? Fungus? Rot? What? Oh, shit, I'm gonna lose them, sure as hell."

I couldn't hold a straight face any longer. I started to giggle, and Markum looked at me suspiciously.

"I'm no medic, Wiggs, but I think you may be digging ashes out of your toes. Shit, man, look around. You're walking around barefoot on a hill that's taken more napalm in the last week than the rest of the 'Nam in the last month. You fucking dingle."

Markum looked around, and then stared at his feet. He licked his thumb, and slowly, as if he thought it would burn him, rubbed at his stained toes. The soot wiped away clean, leaving a fish-belly white streak. His brow clouded over, and I could tell we were in for a pleasant evening of unending bullshit from him. I was saved, for the time being, when Lt. Caplan walked up the hill and started yelling for

Markum to get off his ass and try to raise the firebase. Markum began putting on his socks, jerking them this way and that. He stalked over to where Lt. Caplan and Sgt. Ferris were conferring about something. I walked back to my tree, shaking my head and laughing. That sad, pathetic son of a bitch had just survived eight days of pure hell, and now he was pissed about ashes on his feet. Kind of a twisted world perspective, wouldn't you say?

I sat back down against my tree, thinking about stretching out and catching a few Z's. The residual adrenaline of the last couple of days was beginning to leak out of my system, and I knew the crash would come soon. My eyelids were beginning to grow heavy when a voice right next to me startled me back to wakefulness.

"Well, college boy, we did it again, huh?"

I turned to look at the voice's owner. As always, I had to crane my neck upward to do so. Private First Class Levi Jackson was beyond a shadow of a doubt the single biggest motherfucker I had ever met in my life. He stood six feet, ten inches, and weighed two hundred and ninety pounds, most of which was solid muscle. He was also so black that he almost had an electric blue tint to his skin if the light caught it just right.

Before the army, I had never known a black person, so Levi was a pretty big surprise to me. We had been together since boot camp. I had grown used to the sound of his big, bull-horn voice braying out, "I'm what the Klan fears most, boys, a gigantic nigger with a machine gun", at night before lights out. We had pulled our time in basic, and by some weird stroke of luck wound up in the same platoon in 'Nam. Levi and I were about as tight as two people that aren't blood could get. After the first time I killed a man I got drunk on rot-gut whiskey and cried in his arms. I couldn't imagine doing such a thing now, but I did then, and as I wept in his arms over and over again that I was hell-bound, he had cradled my head and talked to me like you would a tired child. Things like that are hard to explain to people that haven't ever dealt with them first hand, and I get uncomfortable talking about it even to this day. That was Levi and me. He was my brother, closer than the one I had left at home.

"Levi, my man, when we get back to the world, I'm gonna take you to my home town and introduce you to the pleasure that only a white woman can bring."

Levi grinned like a sleepy cat.

"College boy, you can't innerduce somebody that's already acquainted."

I laughed and took out a smoke. I struck fire to my Zippo and lit up. Another thing about Levi I always found odd. The whole time we were in 'Nam, he never smoked a cigarette. Not one. The shit could be flying, shells going off all around us, rounds zipping by with that weird noise that they make, *zzzaaahhhh*-ting!, and there would be Levi, cool as a morgue. I would be puffing away like a madman, but not Levi. We sat in silence for a while, watching the sun start it's decent into the mountains in the west.

After a while, he spoke.

"I'll tell you something, college boy. This fuckin' hill's got the last of me it's gonna get."

Before I could ask him what he meant, he got up and walked into a bunker. I watched him roll his poncho up into a ball and place it under his head. In a few minutes, he was sound asleep. The lucky bastard. A little while later, Sgt. Ferris came by and gave us our watch rotations. I had first watch, so I settled down in my hole and got comfortable.

All this leads up to me, I guess. Sorry it took so long, but I'm not exactly what you'd call a professional writer. First off, my name is Simon Samuels. Corporal Simon Samuels, to be exact. From Hendy's Branch, Kentucky, population 2300. I was a full-time student at the University of Kentucky in the summer of 1968, and doing fairly well. I had a small scholarship, and what little money my folks could send me. Times were tight, but I was getting by. I was keeping my G.P.A. up, and figured to be big-shot lawyer someday.

I was pretty damn tired the night of June 25th. I had just come off an eight hour shift as a busboy at a local family joint, the Blue Barn. All I had on my mind was a shower and a night of coma-like sleep when my roommate Kelly Collins met me at the door.

"Whatchoo doon tonight, Sam-the-Man?"

"I'm going to hit that shower, then hit that bed in a most rigorous fashion", I replied.

"Aw, fuck that, man. Me and Jeff and some of the other guys are going over to Mary's. Come on, it'll be the shit."

Mary's was a seedy bar a few blocks down from the dorm. The mix of farm boys from the outlying area and hippies from the college promised several blood-lettings per night.

"No, thanks, Kelly. I can pass on the vomitorium tonight."

"All, right, bro. Just thought I'd offer. I'll just tell Jessie that you were feelin' a little under the weather..."

I stopped dead in my tracks, my shirt already off and my pants down to my ankles. I was about four steps from the shower.

"Jessie's gonna be there?"

Jessie Stamond was a girl in my Civics class. She was also Pre-law. She was sharp as a tack, and I was sure she was going to make one hell of a lawyer someday. I was also, to wax vulgar, so fuckin' hot for her it hurt. I looked at Kelly with a sly grin.

"Gimme five minutes."

And that was how I wound up in Vietnam.

We arrived at Mary's at ten-thirty. The soldier walked in at eleven-fifteen. Forty-five minutes to change the whole course of my life. My God, sometimes I wish I had taken my shower and gone to bed, fuck Jessie Stamond.

We were all sitting in a corner booth in the back of the bar, listening to Jeff Barnes imitate L.B.J. He was pretty good at it. "I am not gonna send American boys halfway around the world to fuck Vietnamese women that the Vietnamese men should be fucking for themselves", he drawled, eliciting a bray of laughter from us. Over the din, I was talking to Jessie about our Civics class, trying to sound wise and learned. In reality, I was sporting the most massive erection of my entire life. I found it hard to concentrate, because it felt like most of the blood in my body was going into my cock. I would nod sagely at what I hoped were the proper intervals, and then grit my teeth and try to think of anything that would make that fucker go down. Pets I had owned as a child. Teachers I had despised. My grandmother's knitting.

Nothing worked. Old John Thomas just sat there like a stone pole, straining against the fabric of my blue jeans.

I didn't notice the soldier when he first walked in. I had almost succeeded in getting control of my rebellious penis, and was actually carrying on an interesting conversation with Jessie at this point. We were discussing what sort of law we would practice once we passed the bar when Jeff Barnes said, "Well, fuck me backwards. Look'a here."

I looked over at where he was pointing and saw the soldier. He was in his dress uniform, sitting at the bar and drinking Jack Daniel's straight up. Privately, I thought he looked resplendent in his uniform, his medals and ribbons contrasting brightly with the olive drab material. This wasn't the kind of thing you'd say out loud, not at my table. I had been to a few protests, but to be honest, I didn't think much of it. I was going to law school, not Vietnam, so what the hell did it matter to me? Several of the other people at my table felt much more strongly about it, and Jeff was in that crew. He sat staring across the smoky bar at the soldier, muttering to himself. It took me a moment to realize that he was screwing his courage up.

Alarmed, I looked over at Kelly, but he was practicing some amateur gynecology with one of the girls at the end of the table. I turned back to Jeff, meaning to restrain him, but it was too late. He had walked across the bar and was now standing not ten feet from the soldier.

"Hey, baby killer!" he yelled at the soldier's back.

Instantly a hush fell over the bar. All eyes were now riveted on the soldier. With a sigh, he turned and looked at Jeff. His eyes were a mild brown. When he spoke, his voice was soft, much softer than I had expected.

"Can I help you?"

Jeff seemed taken aback. His baby killer had just addressed him in a voice that would have seemed more at home on one of our professors. He sputtered for a few seconds, and then found his voice.

"Taking a little R'n'R from slaughtering innocent civilians, are you? What's that ribbon for? You get more confirmed kills than anybody else in your platoon, or something?"

The soldier's eyes flashed for a half-second. Jeff didn't seem to notice, but I did. It struck home to me that this man had probably killed people. All at once, it was real. This soldier, named Thompson, according to his name badge, was back home from a war. He was trained to kill human beings and that fucking idiot Jeff was standing there, picking a fight with him, for fuck's sake.

Once, when I was eight years old, I was fishing in the river that ran near my house when a black bear walked out of the forest not ten feet from me. It gave me a casual glance, then proceeded to take a drink from the river, turn, and walk back into the forest. The flat gaze of the soldier's eyes elicited the exact same ball-freezing fear I had felt when I had seen that bear. All at once, all I wanted in the world was to be in my dorm room, safely asleep.

The soldier got down from his bar stool and simply stood there, looking at Jeff. After a few moments, he spoke.

"Are you through?"

Jeff once again looked confused. This wasn't going the way he had envisioned it. In the movie reel of his mind, he saw himself confronting this government-sponsored monster, and with a rallying cry from the bar patrons, running him out of Mary's. The monster wasn't reading the same script. He swallowed twice, and began picking at his sleeve. The soldier nodded, as if he had expected this, and continued.

"Good. Now, you'll have to excuse me, but I'm very tired. I just got back from a burial detail. One of my friends. He had requested me to bring his body home, you see. So, if you don't mind, I'm going to sit down at this bar and get drunk enough so I can't hear that fucking twenty-one gun salute in my head anymore. Then, tomorrow, I'm going to get on a plane and fly halfway around the world to fight a filthy war that no one wants so assholes like you can have something to bitch about. So you go back over there with your buddies and drink your drink. You can tell everyone tomorrow about how you faced down an Imperialistic, baby-killing son of a bitch, and struck a blow for the movement, what say?"

Jeff wilted in front of us. He opened his mouth, and then closed it. Opened it again. Closed it. Then, he turned on his heels and walked out of Mary's. I don't know if he expected us to follow him, but we didn't. Conversation resumed around the room, slowly at first, then gaining volume. Ten minutes after the confrontation, the room was just as it had been.

About an hour later, my group began to break up and head to their respective dorm rooms and apartments. Jessie asked me if I wanted to walk her back to her room, but I barely heard her. Getting into Jessie Stamond's pants, once so important, was now trivial. I mumbled some excuse and begged off. I didn't see the hurt look in her eyes as she walked out, but I know it was there. All of my friends had left, and the bar was beginning to empty.

I sat in the corner, drinking my beer and watching the soldier. He hadn't moved an inch since the incident with Jeff, except to raise his drinking arm. As I sat and watched, he drank the entire bottle of Black Jack. I would have been puking and probably on my way to the Medical Center by this point, but the soldier never so much as swayed. I screwed my courage up, and walked over to him. Tapping him on the shoulder was an exercise in courage, all in itself.

"Excuse, me, sir?"

He turned to me, and his eyes were as red as a fire engine.

"I don't mean to bother you", I said, "but I just wanted you to know, I don't think you're a baby killer, or any of that shit."

The soldier smiled wearily and clapped me on the shoulder.

"That's okay, hoss. It's like you fellas say, maybe one day they'll throw a war, and nobody'll show. That would be fine by me, man, just fine by me."

We sat talking about the war for a small while, until the barkeep told us to take our political meeting and hit the road with it. It was only a short time, but the war had taken on a new meaning for me. For the first time, I saw it for what it was. Boys my age were dying halfway around the world while I sat in Civics class and imagined Jessie Stamond and I engaged in the first three chapters of the Karma Sutra. It wasn't right. It wasn't fair. I had been dead on my feet when I had arrived at the dorm earlier that night, but I was rejuvenated. The soldier clapped me on the shoulder again and said, "Keep those grades up, hoss. You lose your Student Deferment, and you'll wind up seeing me again someplace on helluva lot less pleasant." He walked off in an amazingly straight line for someone with his current alcohol intake, turned a corner, and was gone.

I never saw that soldier again. And believe me, I looked.

I walked back to my room. I opened the door to find Kelly Collins lying passed out on the coffee table. His date was lying on the floor next to it. Neither had on any clothes. I picked my way through the living room, hoping that I hadn't really seen semen running off Kelly's stomach onto the coffee table. I went into the kitchen and spent the remainder of the night drinking Jim Beam from a Mason jar.

At first light I took a shower, donned some of my more reputable jeans and a flannel work shirt, and walked out of the dorm. I suppose I could say I was in a blackout, but that wouldn't be true. I was drunk, yes, definitely, but I was also fully aware of what I was doing, and why. I crossed town to the Army recruiter station on Walbash Avenue, signed my name, and smilingly gave my life to Uncle Sam for the next eighteen to twenty months.

I'll spare you the scene at my dorm room later that day. Needless to say, it wasn't pretty. Kelly, whom I had become very close to, damn near punched me in the face when I told him. Word spread like a grassfire, and by three in the afternoon, all my classmates had come by at one point to ask me if I had lost my fucking mind. I smiled, nodded in the right places, and thanked them for their concern.

I felt very calm, almost as if I had taken morphine. I called my parents collect to tell them what I had done. My mother dropped the phone and I heard her go wailing through the house. After a few moments, I heard my father breathing into the receiver. I waited.

"Simon, are you aware of what you've done?"

I considered my answer for a moment.

"Yes, Dad, I am. I'm only doing what you did in Korea, and Papaw did in World War Two. I'm no better than all these other boys that have to go."

He was silent for a while. Finally, he said in a gruff voice that was near tears:

"I went to Korea so you would never have to. Same as your Papaw spent two years hiking across France and Germany to keep me ever having to go. Turns out we were both wrong. Turns out the whole thing was one giant cluster-fuck. We love you, Simon. You call before you leave for Basic."

He hung up. My jaw was somewhere around my sternum. Had I just heard my father utter the words "cluster-fuck"? Yes, by God, I had. I spent most of that evening trying to convince myself that my Pentecostal minister father hadn't used the words "cluster-fuck" in a sentence.

That was how young master Samuels found himself atop Hill 108, in the jolly company of 2nd Platoon. Do I regret it? Sometimes. Would I change it? Probably. *Life is as it is*, as my grandmother used to say, *with naught to be done about it*.

I woke to the sound of Sgt. Ferris' booming voice echoing across the hill.

"C'mon, you lazy fucks, fall in!"

I stretched and blearily gazed across the hill. Dawn was just breaking, and sunlight was beginning to dapple its way across the ground. From fox holes all over the hilltop, men were emerging like Morlocks. We shook the last of the night's damp from our sore bodies and headed over to the small CP that Lt. Caplan and Sgt. Ferris had rigged up in a burned-out bunker. Once we were all accounted for, Lt. Caplan began to speak.

"All right, before I go any further, I don't want to hear any bitching, you guys got that? Zero. None. Nada. Zip. Zilcho. Now, we've just got orders to move out. We're heading across the valley to Hill 122, just over there, to the southwest. An Air Force recon bird thinks they spotted some movement up there, and we're gonna go check it out. So, drop your cocks, grab your socks. Get your gear squared away A.S.A.P. Full kit check in fifteen minutes. Let's move, ladies."

Amid the groans and moans came Levi's voice, very clearly:

"Excuse me, sir?"

"What is it, Jackson?"

"Well, sir, I was jus' wondering who was coming to relieve us here. Don't we need to keep this hill secure until the engineers get here to start work on the firebase?"

"You think to goddamned much, Jackson. All right, may as well tell you now as later. It's been decided by the brass that there isn't a sufficient amount of enemy activity in this sector to justify a firebase. So, yes, ladies, we're off Hill 108 until the next time Charlie digs in.

Now, let's get going. I wanna be on the top of Hill 122 by thirteen hundred hours."

There was a moment of perfect silence. Even the morning birds seemed to be listening. After a pause, Levi, in a soft voice said:

"Nah, sir, I don't think so."

Lt. Caplan did a double take. He looked very closely into Levi's face.

"Jackson, you've got three seconds to be squaring away your gear. If, by the end of that three seconds, you are not squaring your gear, I will have Sgt. Ferris hog-tie you and leave you for the M.P.'s. No, check that, I will have Sgt. Ferris beat the living shit out of you, then hog-tie you and leave you for the M.P.'s. Have you got that, Private?"

Levi never batted an eyelid. A slow, easy smile surfaced on his dirty face.

"Whatever you feel you need to do, L.T., but I ain't givin' this hill back to the Gooks."

Lt. Caplan, was stymied, but only for a second. He wasn't some green college kid that had just got his bars a month ago. He'd been in the shit. He nodded his head and turned to Sgt. Ferris.

"Sergeant, take that man over to the C.P. Discuss this matter with him in a manner you find appropriate."

Sgt. Ferris looked pained, but began to move towards Levi. He had taken about three steps when all hell broke loose.

This is how it happened:

As Sgt. Ferris began walking toward Levi, several of the men moved to his side. Wiggs was one of them. As I may have mentioned, Levi was big. No, nix that, Levi was fucking huge. Sgt. Ferris wasn't going to hesitate one iota, but in my heart, I know that Levi would have dusted his ass. The men at Sgt. Ferris' side were there as back up. Levi never moved, and never lost that dreamy, my-aren't-we-having-fun smile on his face.

I don't know why I did what I did next. People have asked, and I can't answer it any better now than I could have answered it that morning. As they got within arm's reach of Levi, I jerked the charging handle of my M-16. There isn't anything else in the world that sounds like that, and we all knew it by heart. Sgt. Ferris stopped mid-stride and turned to look at me. I looked down at my rifle, unable to believe what I had just done. I'm sure I had a comic "Fuck, guys, don't ask me, the damn thing's crazy" look on my face. Sgt. Ferris said, in a calm voice, "Samuels, I want you to place that rifle on the ground and step away. This don't concern you. Don't go doing something fucked that you'll regret later."

Levi turned to me, and to my utter shock agreed completely.

"College Boy, don' be doin' nothin' stupid. Lissen to Sarge, he's right. This ain't your fight."

Well, friends and neighbors… that got me mad.

"Not my fight? *Not my fight*?? Excuse me, pal, but I'm pretty Goddamned sure that I was right beside you when we climbed this bitch yesterday. I've had it with running up and down this same fucking hill every few months. Fuck that. What about the rest of you guys? You wanna keep trying your luck until one of you gets it in the head next time around? Huh? Henderson? Wallen? What about you, Nicks? If we'd kept this fucker the last time we were here, Botson and Neville wouldn't be in China Beach, and Kenner, Josh, and Paulus wouldn't be going home in fucking flag-draped boxes!"

Their faces looked uncertain. Lt. Caplan walked a few steps closer, but stopped well short of me. He spoke slowly, enunciating each word with painful deliberation, as if speaking to a backward child.

"Samuels, I understand what you're saying, I really do. I don't like climbing this shitheap any more than you do, believe me. If it were up to me, we'd stay right here until our tours were up. But, and I want you to listen carefully, it's not up to me. It's not up to you, either. Or Jackson. The boys at the top want us moving off this hill, and so that's the way it's going to be. Now, how about we forget the last five minutes happened, grab our gear, and be on our merry fucking way?"

To this day, I think the whole confrontation and the frenzied time that followed might have been avoided if Lt. Caplan hadn't uttered that last remark. As he spoke, I had begun to lower my rifle. His voice was soothing, and it made so much more sense than this craziness. Then, his last statement rang in my ears. Lt. Caplan was a lot of things, but forgiving wasn't one of them. He would no more forget this than he would change into black pajamas and start shooting

Americans. Jackson and I had shown red. We weren't to be trusted again, ever. Looking into his eyes, I could see the court-martial and subsequent time in the stockade as if it had already happened. I brought my rifle back up with a snap.

"Sir, if you think I believe that crap, you're crazier than a shithouse rat."

Lt. Caplan's face turned dark red. His eyes began to smolder. First rule of command, never let them get away with giving you shit. Even if "they" in the equation happened to be holding an automatic rifle on you. He suddenly jumped into a roll, grabbing his pistol as he went. I knew what he was going to do, even before he did it. A cold, welcome feeling seeped into my mind. Sound faded out, and it was like looking down a tube. Everything in peripheral vision faded until the only thing I could see was Lt. Caplan. I tracked him with my rifle, the front sight beaded straight at his chest. My arms moved like they were on ball bearings. The sight never wavered, even as he rolled. At that moment, I knew I was going to make the best shot of my life. The shot I killed my own L.T. with. As he came out of his roll, I began applying pressure to the trigger. I had it figured just right. At the same time he rose into a crouch, I was going to send a 5.56 mm shell thundering through the flak jacket he wore, and then on, bursting his heart in his chest.

But that didn't happen.

I think it was because I was in that dark place in your mind that all men go when there is a killing to do that I didn't hear the screams. My whole world was Lt. Caplan. As he came out of his roll, I began applying pressure to the trigger, but the expected crouch never occurred. As I watched in disbelief, Lt. Caplan came off the ground in a gentle arc, rising first up and then out. He moved in slow motion. He didn't look quite right, and after a few seconds, I realized why. His legs were gone. The ends of his fatigues flapped emptily in the wind as he flew.

And then, the rush-roar of returning sound.

I was thrown to my right, both my ears seeping blood. Somehow, I held onto my rifle. I hit the ground hard, and rolled onto my back. Most of the wind had been knocked out of me. As I stared, watching dirt and debris fly across the sky, I wondered just what in the hell had happened. Men were screaming, and sporadic gunfire could be heard all around me. I made it up onto my elbows and looked groggily around.

"What the fuck?"

From over at the C.P., Wiggs, Nicks, and some of the other men that had gone to Sgt. Ferris' side were kneeling, peppering fire across the hilltop. I glanced that way, and saw several of the other men, peppering right back.

"What the *fuck*?!?"

Rounds were zipping back and forth over me, tracers painting their orange-red death across the sky. I might have sat there asking myself what the fuck for several more minutes if it hadn't been for Levi. With shells whipping around him like angry bees, he ran out, threw me over his shoulder like a sack of dog food, and charged back behind an uprooted tree. With a bewildered laugh, I realized this was the same tree I had eaten dinner on the night before. I was holding my rifle by the strap, and it was covered in mud. *Never pass this baby at inspection,* I thought. This brought on another laugh. Levi looked at me like I was an idiot, and then sprayed the C.P. with his M-60. Maybe five minutes since the end of the world, but it felt like much longer than that. I shook my head to clear it, and tried to sit up. Levi shoved me back down, saving my life once again. Several dozen rounds smacked into the tree trunk, throwing a fine spray of splinters and bark into my hair.

As I brushed my face off, I looked at Levi. He had the look of a man determined to eat a dish of his least favorite food, to eat it quickly and get on with his life. He fired an extended burst into the C.P., then ducked back down beside me. I asked once again.

"What the fuck, Levi?"

He smiled at me in a pained way. He jerked his head in the direction of the C.P.

"Corporal "Fucking-Idiot-Asshole" Wiggs back there thought he was gonna be John Wayne. When the shit started to fly, that dumb motherfucker tried to toss a grenade at you. Like we weren't all standing right together, the ignorant fuck. When he tried to lob that bastard, it must've caught on his web gear, or something. All I know is he blew Caplan's fucking legs off. I dunno who started shootin', but a few seconds later, everybody was blastin' everybody. Maybe the fucker thought he'd go up for the Congressional Medal of Shithead, or somethin'."

Levi turned and fired another burst into the C.P. He was rewarded by a high, gobbling shriek. I risked a peek over the tree trunk. Nicks was rolling around on the ground outside the C.P., holding his leg and screaming for a medic. That made me wonder where in the fuck the medic was. I glanced around the trunk to my left, and saw him leaning over Lt. Caplan. As I watched in dumb amazement, Adam Deereborn ran past him and, without pausing, fired a burst into his back. The medic, a decent guy name of Grindhill, went down like a stone. I could see one of his combat boots quiver for a second, then was still.

It dawned on me that everyone on this hill was now acting on pure instinct. A group of nuns would be fair game here. The events of the last few days had caught up with 2nd Platoon with a vengeance. Hell, the war had caught up with us. All the training the army had instilled in us since our first day of boot camp was coming to fruition, albeit not in quite the fashion they had intended.

As I looked at the C.P., I saw Wiggs talking furiously into the field radio. To be more precise, I saw Wiggs' helmet and the radio antenna waggling back and forth. I drew a bead on the radio. You might be asking yourself "Why"? True, I had drawn my weapon against my C.O., but in this day's fuckery, that was a minor infraction, indeed. All I can say is that madness in catching. Probably more so than the flu. You think I'm lying? Explain Germany in 1939 to me, then. Madness, once it gets going, spreads like a grassfire.

The reason I drew a bead on the radio was childish in its simplicity. I didn't want Wiggs telling his side of things first. That's it. The thought of Wiggs telling the brass at the firebase that it was all everyone else's fault filled me with an insanely large feeling of rage. So, I was going to make sure that Wiggs didn't get to tell on us, at least not until we were all telling together.

I didn't mean to shoot Wiggs, I really didn't.

Just as I fired my shot, my well-intended, well-placed shot, Wiggs bent over, I guess to check the map coordinates, or some shit like that. I don't know for sure. As I fired, he leaned just far enough over to take the shot meant for the radio straight through the jaw. His teeth and mandible blew out the other side of his face in a hammer-smash of blood, bone and gristle. As I looked on in horror, something that I first thought was a giant slug worked its way out the hole in his face. Then I realized what it was, and for some odd reason, that filled me with even greater horror and revulsion. One thought streaked across my mind, flashing its neon pattern over and over again.

His tongue, his tongue, oh, fuck me jesus, his tongue,

histonguehistonguehisMOTHERFUCKING TONGUE!!!!!!!!!!

Wiggs threw both of his hands up over his face, mercifully hiding the horrid hole in his jaw. He made weak, clutching gestures at his face, and then, blessedly he slipped out of sight behind the C.P. I dropped my rifle like it was made of molten iron. I curled into a ball, bringing my feet as close to my chest as I could get them. Levi thought I was hit, and was fumbling with me, trying to see where I was bleeding. I heard him, as if from a great distance, yelling at me to show him where I was hit.

The sound of the battle was fading, like some invisible hand was turning the volume down. The world took on a hazy aura, like it was wrapped in sheets of flimsy gauze. The last thing I remember about Hill 108 is how much Levi looked like an angel, a bright halo backlighting him and softening his every feature.

The war in Vietnam ended for me on that day. I woke up under guard in a hospital bed in China Beach. I had suffered a concussion, and was deaf in my left ear. The nurse was checking my blood pressure when I woke up, and after a second she registered that I was looking at her. She gave out a startled little "*Oh!*", and rushed off to find the doctor.

I looked around the room and found a M.P. sitting in a folding chair near the foot of my bed. He said nothing out loud, just stared at me. For a moment, I was scared, thinking he wasn't really there, then he mouthed two words at me. I couldn't hear anything, but I understood perfectly. He said "Goddamn traitor". I was honestly puzzled at that for a moment, and then I remembered what we had done on Hill 108. What I had done. I began crying. The M.P. sat, staring impassively. I didn't try to explain why to him. I doubt he would have understood, since I didn't understand myself.

The next few weeks were spent in a hellish nightmare of questions. I won't bore you with the details. The main question was always why. That, after you boiled it all down, was all they wanted to know. Fuck, truth be told, so did I.

What happened to me? Well, it's nothing that you would figure. I am a prominent lawyer in Lexington, Kentucky. I do quite well for myself. I have a very nice home outside of town on a 38 acre farm. I have a beautiful wife and four wonderful children. After eighteen years of marriage, my wife and I can still look at each other like a couple of high school kids swooning on a first date. I do mostly white-collar cases, but I also do a lot of pro bono work. I know, I know, you're asking yourself *How?* How in the blue fuck can this guy be doing so well? Didn't he just admit to killing one of the men in his own platoon???

The answer is yes, I did. We all did. The war in Vietnam took a horrible turn for the surreal that day. We should have all answered for what happened that day, but none of us did. The few of us that survived were interrogated vigorously, then given discharges and sent back stateside. Honorable discharges, by the way. In any other world, we would have all hung for the mutiny on Hill 108.

Our saving grace was the fact that Hill 108 fell on the right of the line instead of the left. Brass couldn't very well prosecute us for committing these crimes in Vietnam, not when we were in Laos when they occurred. Yeah, we got away with it, not because we covered our tracks, not because we destroyed the evidence, but because good old Rand McNally said we were a few miles into another country. You have to love it when the underdog beats the system, don't you?

So, here I am. Like I said, I do well, and I'm a basically happy guy. I kept up with Levi after we got back. He was killed in a bar fight. Four men jumped him and stabbed him thirty-seven times. I didn't go to the funeral. I felt like a coward, but I honestly didn't think I could handle the sight of Levi lying in a flag-draped coffin. It felt like a cheat. I couldn't get rid of the sneaking suspicion that my M.P. would be there, sitting in the back, unchanged even after nearly twenty years. I was terrified that he would be sitting there, and he would look at me with those flat, dead eyes and mouth two words.

Vietnam has become a distant memory to me now. I never have flashbacks. I don't drink too much. I enjoy my life. I love my wife and my kids. I do what I can to improve myself. If I wake up every few months screaming *His tongue! His tongue!*, so what? If that's the only price I have to pay, I'll gladly pay it.

But God, oh, God, I'm so afraid that the price will be so much more.

The Green Man

He tried to raise his head, but the weight of it overpowered the underdeveloped muscles of his scrawny neck. He was forced to contend with this fact, and let his head flop back against his breastbone, his eyes dazed and hopeless.

It was nearly time for the Green Man to come. He could tell by the way the light from the sun had climbed up the far wall through the barred windows. Allowing for the change of the seasons, the bar of light would be about three-quarters of the way up the wall when Green Man came today. It would be as it was every time he was forced to deal with Green Man. First, the cajoling, pleading, and altogether infuriatingly logical attempt to get him to talk.

After he remained silent for a half-hour, Green Man would then sigh and shake his head sadly. Green Man would ask why his inmate must make things so very difficult for himself, when a simple sentence would end all this pain, all this sorrow. When he received no answer, Green Man would raise his eyes theatrically to the heavens and ask God "Why this, my Lord? Why does this man make me cause him such suffering? Does he not know how heavy this weighs on my heart, this pain I must inflict?" His performance done, he would walk back out of the tiny concrete room and step into the hall. A few moments later, he would return, pushing before him a wheeled cart covered with an olive drab blanket.

Each day, there would be something new under the blanket. Even after so many days, Green Man had always managed to come up with something new with which to torture and unhinge him. It was amazing, really, that in all this time Green Man had never repeated himself. Even if the horrors under the blanket were of a similar theme to one he had used before, they were never exactly the same.

Although he couldn't know it, Green Man was giving his captive something to occupy his mind with. He had made a game of it, trying to guess what the blanket would reveal each day. Would it be spiders today? No, of course not. Green Man had used scorpions just a week prior, and spiders would be too close for comfort. Perhaps Green Man might return to what appeared to be his favorite theme of all, surgical tools of various makes and models. Whatever the blanket uncovered, it was certain to be horrifying and painful. But that was of little consequence. Horror and pain were things that no longer held any interest for the captive.

You see, Green Man didn't know it, but the captive could no longer feel anything from his neck down. He could move, and was in complete control of his musculature, but as the weeks had turned to months, the months to years, the incessant pain had caused his nerve endings to simply stop sending their starbursts of panicked messages to his brain. So Green Man didn't catch on, the captive would scream accordingly when the daily horror was placed on his skin.

The captive enjoyed having this little secret from Green Man. It gave him a sense of being higher on the cosmic scale than his torturer. Not that it would take much to fulfill that requirement. The captive had met many, many rats in his cell that were above Green Man in the wheel of the cosmos.

As the captive watched, the bar of sunlight rose to the mental mark he had placed on the wall. Exactly on time, the key rattled in the lock and Green Man entered. Punctual as always, Green Man walked into the room and squatted down in front of the captive. His voice dripping with concern, he asked, "Is today the day you end our mutual torment, my friend? I must confess to you, I am beginning to worry about us both. You are in danger of losing your mind. I am in danger of losing my soul if I must continue to cause you this unspeakable pain. Please, my friend, tell me what it is I need to know, and let us end this horror, together."

The captive raised his eyes and met Green Man's gaze. With a slow smile, he shook his head exactly three times, and then lowered his chin back onto his chest. He could hear Green Man huff and blow. The captive hid a smile. He knew what that those sounds were a precursor to a full-bore rant from Green Man. Those were always entertaining. Of course, the pain would be double, if not treble what it usually was after one of these, because Green Man did not like to lose his composure. The captive was very glad that he no longer felt pain.

"Why?" shouted Green Man, "Why do you do this to yourself, to me? Can you not see how painful this is for me? Thinking only of yourself, so selfish you are! It is not you that must shoulder this burden! No, you take your punishment and then sit there, feeling superior, while I must take with me the memories of your screams, the stench of your burnt flesh! Do you, *can* you, imagine what it is like for me at my home, sitting at dinner with my children, making love to my wife? Times that I should feel nothing but the bliss and satisfaction of a man who's duty has been done, instead I feel as if I should shower over and over again, if only to wash the stink of this cell from my skin! Do you care? Of course not! You sit there in your righteous condemnation of me, I who only do as duty requires! Why? Have you run mad? I am beginning to believe that *I* have run mad! I cannot continue this forever. You must tell me what I need to know, and you must do so soon! I will not abide this any longer, do you hear me? *DO YOU???*"

His rage spent, Green Man stood in the center of the tiny cell, his breath screeching in and out of his chest. The captive raised his head as much as possible and looked Green Man in the eyes. With another smile, he shook his head three times, and then closed his eyes again.

Green Man went wild with rage. He stalked back and forth across the cell, kicking at the floor and pulling at his hair. He spoke in incoherent spats, mixing words and phrases into a long line of gibberish. Suddenly coming to a stop in the center of the cell, he wrenched his pistol from his holster and pointed it at the captive.

Hearing the creak of leather as the gun left the holster, the captive raised his head fully, a Herculean effort. He stared into the eyes of Green Man, his eyebrow arced quizzically. Green Man stood pointing the pistol at the captive, a vein bulging prominently on his forehead. With a savage grunt, Green Man holstered the weapon.

"Oh, you'd like that, wouldn't you? You'd like nothing more than to have me condemn my soul to Hell for your murder! Well, push it from your mind! It will never happen, do you hear me? *Never*!!!"

The captive lowered his head again. Green Man resumed his pacing, back and forth, back and forth. He covered miles inside the confines of the tiny cell. The bar of sunlight had now risen to its highest mark on the wall. The hours passed, and yet Green Man did not exit the cell and return with his cart of horrors. The captive sat unmoving, wondering what this new turn of events would bring. Never before had Green Man acted in so odd a manner. He could be as warm as Father Christmas, or as cold as the snowy climes in which that fabled man lived.

He could be convincing, threatening, brotherly, or sinister as the mood took him. He was a Harlequin, a Janus mask, a shape-shifter that howled at the moon. But until this day, he had never been…

frightened? Was *that* the word? Could it be that Green Man was genuinely

bending under the immense pressure put on him by his superiors to

glean information from the captive? The captive raised his eyes again

and gave a long, thoughtful, speculative glance at Green Man.

Yes, there were signs that Green Man was under a great deal of

stress. His clothing, usually so immaculate and pressed with creases

sharp enough, to cut seemed slept-in and rumpled. His hair, close-cut

on the sides and combed with perfection to the right was in slight

disarray, with spikes shooting up here and there like dandelions in a

freshly cut field of grass. His usually smooth face was covered in

stubble, not enough to call even a five o'clock shadow, but enough to

be noticeable. Yes, it was possible that Green Man might be coming

unhinged. The thought of that filled the captive with a warm sense of

accomplishment. He lay his head back on his chest and closed his eyes

to better bask in that warm glow as Green Man paced, back and forth,

back and forth.

Hours passed. Several times, the underlings of Green Man

came to the cell door to see if anything was amiss. Green Man screamed and growled at them, and they disappeared as if by magic. Daylight faded, and night drew upon the land. The single bare light bulb in the captive's cell flickered weakly and then burned brightly, casting harsh shadows over the cell. In the defining light, Green Man began to look more and more like White Man as all the color fell from his face. He had stopped addressing the captive directly hours hence and now only spoke to himself in brief, incoherent bursts. Finally, as the night was giving way to the coming dawn, Green Man slid down the wall opposite the captive and sat staring at him with glazed eyes.

"Why?" asked Green Man, his voice so soft that the captive could barely make it out. "Why do you do this? More to the point, *how* do you do this? How can you bear this, day after day? Why haven't you broken? They all break, you know. It takes some longer than others, but in the end, they all break. All but you. How is this?" Green Man's voice was plaintive, his eyes desperate with confusion. "How are you so different?"

The captive looked at Green Man and smiled. Then he shook his head three times. Slowly. Inexorably. Three times, no more, no less.

Green Man began to shake. It was a slight tremor at first, coursing up and down his body like the electricity he had often used on the captive. Within minutes, the tremor had evolved into spasms. Green Man convulsed against the wall, his head beating a tattoo against the cold, wet stone. A fine spray of saliva began to form at the corners of his mouth, and soon became large ropes of white froth that splattered the floor, the walls, Green Man's clothing. After the worst of the convulsions had ceased, Green Man lay half on his side, moaning, his eyes rolled up to the whites. He lay like that for a long time.

The sun rose and began its daily trek up the wall. As the captive watched, the bar of light rose slowly over Green Man. When the bar reached Green Man's eyes, they snapped open like window blinds. Green Man sat up with a start, sitting with military precision, his back ram-rod straight, his shoulders back. He looked at the captive with eyes that showed nothing more than madness… a hopeless madness. His voice cracked as he asked the captive his question again.

"Will you talk now? Will you tell me what I need to know?"

The captive smiled and shook his head three times.

Green Man pounced to his feet and stood at attention. He gave the captive a crisp salute, and then pulled the pistol from the holster. With no hesitation, Green Man placed the barrel of the weapon in his mouth and pulled the trigger. The noise was muffled by Green Man's mouth, but still loud enough to echo crazily in the confines of the tiny cell. Green Man's brains exited his skull with a wet smack against the stone behind him. He dropped like a rotted cow hide, his limbs arranged in impossible angles. The cell filled with the stench of feces as Green Man voided himself. Green Man twitched slightly once, twice, thrice... and then lay still.

The captive watched all this with a clinical detachment. Reaching up with one hand, he scratched his head. This was the most movement he had exhibited since Green Man's entry into the cell the previous day. The manacles that held him in place against the wall rolled down his emaciated arm all the way to the elbow. With careful and considered movements, the captive slowly stood.

Had someone told Green Man that the captive was capable of such a feat yesterday, he would have laughed until tears flooded his cheeks. Lowering his arms, the captive allowed the manacles to fall from his skeletal arms to the floor with a clatter. Totally unfettered, the captive walked slowly to where Green Man lay in his own filth, his eyes black with hemorrhages. The captive leaned carefully over, making sure not to overbalance and disturb Green Man's rest. His voice rusty and metallic from disuse, he whispered into Green Man's blood-clotted ear.

"The answer is… *I don't know.*"

The captive straightened and began his slow shuffle towards the unlocked door. Alarms rang out all over the building as men ran to and fro, trying to ascertain the location of the shot. None of them gave a second glance to the emaciated scarecrow of a man that walked unhurriedly towards the front gate, and then through it. The captive, no longer in captivity, shuffled down the road under the palm trees that lined it. He raised his face to the sun, feeling its warming rays for the first time in years. The breeze was clean and fragrant with flowers.

The man who had been the captive walked down the road and into his freedom.

The Broken Man

The broken man lay on a ledge of cold rock, his face turned to the cloud-blotted sun.

His eyes shone out between tendrils of whipping hair, bright blue glints that stared unblinkingly into the desolate sky. His face was covered in dried blood, cracked and flaking. Hands bound by frozen iron rings clenched into fists until small runnels of fresh blood coursed down his wrists. From his manacles of iron ran a length of chain half the length of a man fastened at the end into the very stone itself. Bare were his feet, exposed to the biting North wind that blew constantly.

Of raiment he had little, clothed only in filthy rags that flapped about his spare frame. All about him the ledge bore red, testament to the horrific trials brought forth upon him. Here and there shone bright spots of color, fecal matter of the ravens that even then stood mute watch over him. At times one or more of them would swoop down onto his stone bed and peck at his shattered body. Torn as he was, he continued to fight them off, but they, sensing his death, grew brave and bold, and would not fly far as they had in the beginning.

The broken man lay on his ledge of cold rock, his face still turned to the cloud-blotted sun.

This was his torment, this, his penance, his trial. He was and remained unsure of his crime, knowing only that it must have been great, indeed, to deserve such swift and terrible retribution. For on his rock lay the very keys to his shackles. One on the left, wrought of pure gold, the other on his right, crafted of the purest of silver. Both keys would fit the lock, both would free him with but a turn from his torment. Lying at the foot of the rock was a chest that contained both food and clothing, and gold enough to see him safely home in comfort. Such a small matter, the turning of a key. For days on end he would stare at the keys, first one then the other, a stricken look of the most horrible misery on his face.

Why would the man stare at his salvation and do nothing about it, you ask?

In his prison he remained, for the handiwork of his warders was of the most ill-design. Should he choose the golden key, no more than he had turned the lock, then would his wife fall dead, struck as if from a clear sky. Should he choose the key of silver, then it would be his daughter that would find death upon her with swift, silent wings. His love for them both, this was his true warden.

The broken man lay on his ledge of cold rock, his face even

now turned to the cloud-blotted sun.

The wind snaked across him, around him, through him. It froze his very bones. The ravens gave voice to a terrible cry, shrill and rending.

The broken man turned his face from the cloud-blotted sun as his last breath issued forth from his lips in a long sigh.

His eyes closed. He saw no more. He felt no more. He was no longer the prisoner, no longer the slave.

The broken man lay dead on his ledge of cold stone.

Upon his lips lay a smile of sweetest release.

His love was safe.

The No-Fun Club

Everyone knows that no matter what the culture, there is a myth about how death befalls us all. From Judeo-Christianity to Shinto, from Islam to Buddhism, every people, of every country have a specific tale that relates to death. And no matter what form that death takes, it has one pretty central theme: it's permanent. Now, there are of course several religions that espouse the notion of reincarnation, but that's not what I'm talking about. Death, when it comes for the physical body, is permanent, at least to that body. Whether the soul migrates on to an afterlife or comes back as a brand new human being is moot. The body you inhabit right now, this second, is dying, and will, in due time, cease to exist. The life functions will cease and within seconds after you stop breathing, bacteria will begin their assault on your now-inert form. Without preservative measures, your body will become unrecognizable to your family and friends within days. Parasitic organisms will begin to devour your flesh, and will continue, unabated, until there is nothing left but bone.

Nice little thought to begin with, isn't it? The absolute fact that you are nothing but a bag of meat and bone that will rot and turn into putrescent worm-food is enough to brighten anyone's day, don't you think? But hey, it happens to us all. Or so I'm told. Personally, I've been dead since 1944, and I'm still very much in the upright and un-rotted position. Not a maggot to be found, no sagging flesh, no wretched stench that could drive off a hobo with a pet skunk. A rabid pet skunk with chronic halitosis, at that. No, I am, insofar as I can tell, I am a one hundred percent walking, talking, one hell of a flamingo-dancing human being. I'm just not alive. I'm not a vampire, or anything like that, before you start jumping to conclusions. But if I *was* a vampire, it would be a *real* vampire, one that jumped out in the night and ate your ass, not one that was all soulful and shimmered like Rainbow Brite in the sun. Jesus, how I loathe what those books and movies have done to good old-fashioned vampires. Give me Bela Lugosi over Eddie Van Cullen any day. Sorry about that remark. I just totally cheapened the good name of Van Halen, and for that I tender my most heartfelt apologies. Won't happen again, scout's honor.

Anyway, I think I was trying to tell you about the little hang-up I have about being alive before I went off on that vampire tangent. It's simple, really. You, the reader, for example are alive. You breathe, eat, excrete, sleep, and if you're very lucky, have sex on occasion. I, the writer of this little missive on the other hand, am dead. I neither breathe nor eat, excrete nor sleep. Although if I'm very lucky, I do get to have sex occasionally. So, we're not all that far apart, when you think about it, right?

I believe I may be telling this story a bit backwards. Let me try to tackle this from a different angle. You are no doubt at this point scratching your head and wondering why in the hell you shelled out good money to read something that seems to have been written by someone in dire need of their daily medication. If so, I applaud you, because that's about how I feel writing it. So, let's back-track a bit and try to cover some of the salient points that brought about my complete lack of being alive-ness, shall we?

I was 23 years old in 1944. Like most able-bodied men, I was in the service. There was a little skirmish you might have heard of going on at the time. They called it "World War Two", because "World War One" had already been taken, and "Are You *Shitting* Me? *Again*???" didn't seem to have the right ring to it. Anyway, I was in the Army, along with just about everyone else I had ever met in my life. I didn't notice my Grandma at Basic, but she may have been on a different base than me. While in Basic Training, I was given training that was very basic. One thing I loved about Army life in the 40's was that there wasn't a lot of imagination involved in the naming of things. A shovel became an "Entrenching Tool, Personal, G.I. Issue, Property of the U.S. Army", and a set of clothes became "Uniform, M-1943, HBT, G.I. Issue, Property of the U.S. Army". Concise and to the point, just the way I liked it. And much the way you would undoubtedly like for me to continue this story.

So, 23 years old, an American Soldier, out to give old Uncle Adolph one in the eye for God, Mom, and Apple Pie. With me so far? That's good, but to tell the truth, my mom's apple pie wasn't all that good. Let's just skip ahead a tiny bit to June of 1944. Yeah, I know, you can see this one coming. And yes, I was aboard one of the landing craft rocking and rolling its way towards Omaha Beach that happy June 6th day. But this is where I'm going to pull a fast one on you and *not* tell you about how I single-handedly wiped out several German pillboxes and made it possible for our boys to establish a beachhead that morning before succumbing to multiple gunshot and stab wounds from my ferocious hand-to-hand combat. In fact, I didn't find out what happened in Normandy until later, when a man filled me in on the details. But more about that later.

No, what happened to me was much, much braver and more tragic than anything like that. What actually happened was that when the landing craft ramp lowered, I surged ahead with everyone else aboard, took three lunging steps into the waist-high Atlantic Ocean, and got shot right through the head by a German manning a *Maschinengewehr 42*, or as our boys called it, the MG-42, or "Hitler's buzzsaw". The MG-42 was a belt-fed machine gun that fired between 1,200 and 1,500 7.52x57 mm rounds per minute. Not that all of that information is pertinent, but then again, *you* didn't take one of those damned rounds right above your left eye, now did you? It leaves a lasting impression, and makes one a bit obsessive when it comes to knowing all about the weapon that killed you. As a matter of fact, I also happen to know the name of the German who shot me. His name was Gunther Spieglemann, 18 years old, from Dusseldorf, and he didn't outlive me by more than an hour. A grunt with a Tommy gun slid into the back of Gunther's pillbox and plugged him with about twenty .45 ACP rounds. What goes around comes around, Gunther. Sometimes you eat the bear, and sometimes the bear sneaks up behind you and blasts you out of your jackboots. Although eighteen is awfully young to be blown out of footwear of any kind, if you ask me.

Okay, you're now asking (if you've been paying attention, that is), "Hey, Narrator, if you had your brains blown into the Atlantic Ocean on D-Day, as you would have us believe, then how are you writing this entirely confusing narrative?" Well, I was getting to that if you would just cool your jets for a minute. Where were we? Ah, yes, with me bobbing gently in the sea, the back of my head ripped away. At least I assume that's what it looked like. From my standpoint, it happened like this: The ramp dropped, I moved forward with all the other guys, I took those aforementioned lunging steps landward, and there was a massive *crack!* from inside my head, I saw a swirling blackness, and then… I found myself standing in Central Park, New York City, United States of America. And I have to add here that it is a testament to the changing times that although I received a few sideways glances, no one stopped to ask why there was a man in wet combat fatigues with a Garand rifle (or, if you prefer, a "U.S. Rifle, Caliber .30, M1) with full bandoleers of ammo standing in Central Park with a very confused look on his face. I can only guess that folks must have thought, "Hell, there's a war on, maybe this is one of the new precautions the military is taking to keep the dreaded Hun from our shores." (Although how one man with a rifle was supposed to hold Central Park against the Wehrmacht is beyond me.) Nowadays, a man standing in Central Park with a pocket knife is subject to seizure and arrest. The times, they are a changin' my friends.

So, from having my head turning into a taco just off the French coast to standing in Central Park in an instant… enough to confuse just about anyone, wouldn't you agree? It sure confused the hell out of me. I had no idea what to do, so I just stood there in a sort of half-assed parade rest, looking stupid. That seemed to help enormously, because after a few minutes a large man in a business suit walked up to me and said, "Son, we need to talk. Would you mind following me? This isn't exactly the best place to have this conversation."

Why not, I thought. *I just got shot in the head in France, you know. I'm up for just about anything.* Without another word, he did a neat about-face and headed across the park at a brisk rate. We crossed the park and came upon a large hotel. The concierge gave me the stink-eye for dripping water onto his nice marble floor, but at least it was well-traveled French water. The big man in the suit asked for his room key and we ambled over to the elevator. I wasn't really surprised when we got out at the top floor, and the man used his key to open the penthouse suite. He gestured for me to enter politely and held the door open for me.

We entered the living room and I let out a low whistle. This was a far cry from the tent city I'd been living in over in England before the invasion. This place looked like a palace. The man inclined his head towards a large leather chair and asked me to have a seat.

"Oh, I can't sit there, sir", I blurted. "I'm soaked and covered in sand and blood... I'd ruin that chair. I can just stand here, this is fine."

The man gave me a quizzical glance and flapped his hand at me. My arms suddenly felt like they were going to float up by themselves and after a second I understood why. My Garand was gone, along with all my ammo. Oh, and all my disheveled clothing, as well. That bears mentioning. In their place, I was now attired from head to toe in a stunning suit almost identical to the one my companion was wearing. He gave me a considering look and then nodded. "Something to drink?" he asked. I may have mentioned I was a soldier, and one of the very first things I learned once I got out of Basic Training was that you never, *ever*, turn down a drink, so I promptly said, "Yes, sir, whisky straight up, if you please." The man gave me an odd little grin but marched over to the bar and poured several fingers of what turned out to be very nice Scottish whisky in a glass and hand it to me. I downed it and smiled like a schoolboy that would like another piece of pie for dessert.

At this point, my companion laughed. It was deep and seemed like it should have been frightening, but I simply found it catching, and laughed right with him. He took my glass from my hand and started to pour me another, thought better of it, and just handed me the glass and bottle both. "God bless you, sir", I said sincerely. "You are truly one of the chosen few." He motioned me back to the seat. Seeing as I was now dressed like a movie star and in possession of a fine bottle of Scottish whisky, I saw no reason not to have a seat. I got comfortable and poured myself another drink. Had I *really* been in a Higgins boat off the coast of France an hour or so ago?

My companion took a seat at a desk not far from my chair and folded his hands together and looked at me expectantly. Noticing his stare, I said quickly, "Again, thank you very much, sir. You have no idea how much this hits the spot. I haven't had a decent whisky since…" I trailed off, trying to remember the name of the pub in Brighton that my friends and I had visited. The man coughed to get my attention.

"First, and foremost", he said, "I won't have you calling me 'Sir'. I don't care for it, to be honest, and it's been a very, very long time since anyone called me the equivalent. So, if you don't mind, please call me Caelius."

I gave him a confused look which he bore patiently. Finally, I found my tongue again and was able to ask, "Uh…sir? Oh, sorry…uh, Caelius, I'm not sure I understand much of anything you just said. I mean, I understand the words, I speak English just fine, but as far as the actual *content* of what you said…I'm a little hazy."

He smiled and sat back in the big chair behind the desk. He tilted his head up towards the ceiling and closed his eyes. Taking a large breath, he began speaking. He had no real discernable emotion in his tone; he could have been giving a stock report. He said, "First, to proper introductions. It is unforgivable of me to have been so crude as to have not done so before, but I felt it more pressing to make haste in getting you out of public view and getting you more properly attired. I hope you do forgive me?" Here he cocked an eye toward me. I nodded vigorously. Smiling again, he resumed his position, facing the ceiling with closed eyes and continued in a monotone.

"My name is Decimus Titus Caelius. I was born in the year 35 B.C., as you reckon time. I served the Emperor Caesar Augustus from the year 14 B.C. until the year 9 A.D., again as you reckon time. We did so differently then, having never heard of the man you call Jesus Christ, ergo we were given no notice of any "B.C.-A.D" changeover. So, yes, before you ask, I am a hair under one thousand, nine hundred and seventy-nine years old. I was only alive for forty-two of those years, however. I was killed in the Teutoburger Wald by a warrior from the Cheruci. You would know it as the Battle of the Teutoburg Forest. In 9 A.D. General Publius Quinctilius Varus took three legions into the forest to put an end to the Germanic threat growing there. The area had been declared 'pacified', and Varus was given governorship of all Germania. Before that he had been the governor of Africa and later, of Syria. He was not well-liked." Caelius looked at me askance and said, "Did you know that during the Jewish uprisings in Judea after the death of Herod, Varus crucified two thousand Jews?" I shook my head solemnly. He looked back at the ceiling and continued.

"We were three legions, so we figured on a very short campaign. Fifteen thousand troops against a rag-tag band of rabble that had already been pacified? Most of us didn't even see the point, to speak truthfully. The three legions were the *Legio* XVII, *Legio* XVIII, and *Legio* XIX. That's Seventeenth, Eighteenth, and Nineteenth Legions to you, as I believe Latin is not in your everyday vocabulary."

I interrupted. It wasn't intentional, just a knee-jerk reaction. "Show me someone that has Latin in their everyday vocabulary, and I'll show you some brainy geek that's manning a desk instead of a rifle." Realizing what I had just said, and how insulting it must have sounded, I looked at Caelius with terror-stricken eyes. To my relief, he was smiling and not jumping over the desk to rip my recently healed head off. I think I mentioned he was large. I'm not small by any standards, 5'10", but Caelius was easily over 6'6', and had the muscle to back it. Instead of killing me (again), he just continued.

"You speak truly. My language has fallen out of favor, except with those among the educated and those that wish to *appear* so. At any rate, our three legions were far in excess for the mission, or so we thought. The Greeks would have called it *hubris*, I believe, and rightfully so."

"I was the *Primi Ordines* of the *Primi Cohort* of the *Legio Septima Decima*." He grinned at me mischievously, which dissolved into a laugh. "That means I was a high-ranking officer of the First Cohort of the Seventeenth Legion."

"What's a *Cohort*?"

"A *Cohort* was eight hundred men, or five double-strength *Centuries*."

"And what are *Centuries*?"

Here he finally gave me a look of slight aggravation. "Listen carefully, because my purpose here is not to give you a lesson on Roman military structure. However, if it will end your questions, I'll give you a quick overview. First, the *Legio*. Made up of officers, men, engineers, and sometimes cavalry, or *equites*. There were usually about five thousand, four hundred men in each *Legio*. In each of these *Legio* were around seven *cohorts*. Each of these *cohorts* had about four hundred and eight men, and each *cohort* was led by one man. A cohort was made up of six *Centuriae*, with eighty men in each, with one man in charge of each *Century*. There were almost seven *cohorts* in each *Legio*. Each *Centuriae* was commanded by a *Centurion*, who had as his second-in-command an *Optio*, which was like a Lieutenant, and a *Tesserararius*, who was like a Sergeant. Now, is that clear enough for you?"

I grinned at him. "Hell, yes, that's clear enough for me. You could have just said, 'We had three Regiments, which were made up of seven battalions, which were made up of six companies. See, that wasn't so hard, *and* I didn't have to speak anything but English."

Again, I realized that my tone just *might* be taken the wrong way. Taken the wrong way by a very large, and to hear him tell it, very old man. Not that he resembled Grandpa in any way. I kept the grin plastered to my face and hoped he was as patient as he was large. Thankfully for me, he was. He just smiled a little, one corner of his lip raising slightly, and then returned to his head-back, eyes-closed posture.

He continued, "So there we were, three legions out to pacify an already "pacified" people. We thought it to be a joke, really, until we were set upon by thirty thousand screaming Cheruuci led by Arminus.

Arminus had become close to Varus, and had lived in Rome for a time. However, it seems his first loyalty was to his people. I can't blame him, really. The actions of the ruling class in Germania, as they did in other provinces, caused wide-spread hunger and anger."

"We were strung out in a single line, thousands of meters long, along a single muddy trail that led through the forest. A horrible storm arose, and we soon found ourselves slipping in mud, trying to retain our footing. The fog was so thick that soon it was impossible to see the man in front of you clearly. Everything was wrapped in gauze. We were miserable, wet, and cold. The men were grumbling, and I could hear voices coming out of the mist, angry and tired. I felt just the same. I would have been more apt to follow an ass into battle than Varus, for I felt he was what you would call 'full of himself'. But I was a commanding officer, and my place was to assert authority over those under my command, and I had orders to follow."

"Orders. I had orders, the gods save me… orders."

Caelius paused, unmoving. I had no idea what to do or say, so I remained silent and waited for him to continue. After what seemed like forever, he did.

"They came out of the fog on all sides of us. Before we were even aware an attack was underway, the massacre had already begun in earnest. I lost most of my men before I was able to even begin to organize a column. Imagine it, if you will, this forest Hell. Dark, gloomy, a storm raging about us like the gods themselves were bent on our death, covered in cold mud and hot blood in equal parts."

"The civilian camp followers that accompanied us were shown no more mercy than those of us in uniform. All were slaughtered equally. I was in the process of trying to rally my remaining troops when I was attacked by four Cheruci. I dispatched three of them with my gladius, but in the melee the fourth had managed to slip behind me."

"Now, you are a soldier, albeit one of low rank, so you know the importance of strategy. In a torrential rainstorm, with the screams of dying all about me, four bearded barbarians who wanted nothing less than my head on a spike, strategy was a thing hard come by. I fell back on my training, as all soldiers do, but the men that I called to arms did not arrive, for they were in the same situation as myself. They were fighting and dying alone, just as I was.

"The thing that made the Roman Army the most formidable of its day was organization. No other army had it, or if it did, it was a pale shadow to the organization that we had. Our enemies would attack us without any cohesion, without strategy, just a disorganized mass of screaming men. When this charge would strike our lines, they would crumble. They simply could not break through the ranks. Each legionary would be in a line, and would fight until a whistle blew, they would fall back and allow the man behind them to take up the fight. Thus, there were always fresh men at the front line. Our adversaries would fight on, until their fatigue would cause them to grow weary and make a mistake, at which point our men would kill them. The system was efficient, and it made us an Empire."

This system, however, could not be brought to bear in this instance. Arminius knew that Varus had strung out our lines, and used this to his advantage. He had made alliances with the other tribes, so we found ourselves facing not a pacified land with a handful of rabble, but a vast army. We stood no chance. They massacred over twenty thousand Romans. But even with the surprise of the ambush, the inability to form our lines as we normally would, it still took them three days to finish us. I find some solace in that. That, plus the fact that

Varus fell on his own sword once defeat seemed inevitable. Even for a fool such as he, a clean Roman death was preferable to having a General fall into the hands of the Germanic horde."

"I spoke of the fourth Cheruci that had slipped behind me during my battle with the other three. I turned to fight him. I don't remember the blade sliding into my back, but I do remember the blood rushing down my right leg and pooling on the ground. I remember how warm it was, and strangely enough, how good it felt to be warm, if only for a moment."

"I remember drawing back my blade to kill the Cheruci, for he was unarmed, his blade still stuck in my back. I remember thrusting forward, but whether the blow landed and I received my vengeance, I do not know, for blackness fell across my vision and I felt nothing more. Then, just as you, I came to myself someplace completely different than I had been only seconds before."

"I came to my senses unharmed, yet confused. At first, I thought I was blind, for I could see nothing but a great white glare. After a few moments, this faded, and I found myself standing in bright, hot sunlight. After the Teutoburg Forest, this was about as different a surrounding one could find. I told you of the heat and the glare, but there was also the smell. The forest had a musty, wet odor, whereas now I could smell dry, spiced sand. I was, as I said, confused."

"It turns out I was in a village called Dehenet, or as the Greeks called it, Akoris, Egypt. I stood in the village square, much as you did, simply waiting to see what would happen next. I knew I had died in the forest, and yet this did not look like any afterlife I had grown up learning of. I would not have thought Elysium to be quite so hot and sandy. I was given many strange stares by those in the square, but none seemed too quick to approach, as I was still armed and covered in mud and blood. A wise choice, for I was confused, and in me, confusion and fear lead me to attack without much forethought. I was impetuous in those days."

"Finally, a young woman of great beauty walked directly up to me. She never even gave my sword a glance. In perfect Imperial Latin she said to me 'Greetings, Roman. I am called Nefertari. I imagine you have questions, do you not?' Of course she was right. I had questions, thousands of them, and she knew the answers to each one. I had questions that I imagine you have now, yourself. So, where shall we start? I already know more about you than you can possibly imagine, but I find that it is best perhaps if you speak to me now of your life. Then I will answer all the questions you have. Does this suit you?"

I sat silently for a moment, absorbing all this and drinking whisky. It hadn't really dawned on me until that instant that I had just assumed I was dead and this was a Purgatory of sorts. An odd Purgatory, but Purgatory nonetheless. Not being able to think of a better place to start, I asked just that.

"All right, Caelius, is any of this real? Am I dead on the beach in France and this is Purgatory? Or am I maybe dreaming all this? For all I know, I'm asleep on my bunk back in Tent City in England, waiting for orders."

Caelius smiled and said, "Answers to all that a bit later. As I said, tell me of yourself first. Then I will 'fill you in', as they say."

I tossed my hands in the air, unmindful of the whisky in one of them, and blew out an exasperated breath. When I spoke, my voice had taken on a slight edge.

"Fine. My name is Johnathon Levi Anderson, Private First Class, Serial Number 273-88-7868. I was born In Bluejacket, Oklahoma on March 3rd, 1921. I lived on a farm, just like everyone else, worked cattle, went to school, graduated, joined the Army, became a soldier, went to France, and got killed. Anything else? I mean beside the fact that apparently that last bit is off, since I somehow managed to get my fucking head blown off in France, but now I'm sitting in a place that looks like a king's palace talking to a very strange man that has told me a great deal without telling me anything at all. *Sir.*"

Caelius grimaced slightly at that last "sir", but bore the rest patiently. He simply looked at me, silent. I tried to glare back at him, but my will broke and my eyes dropped to the floor between my feet. When I finally spoke again, it was barely a whisper.

"And I'm scared. I don't understand what's happening to me, and I'm scared. There. Are you happy now?"

I tried to hold them back, but I couldn't help it. I watched as two teardrops fell towards my immaculate shoes. I have no idea how he moved so fast, so *silently*, but Caelius was there before the drops had struck.

He knelt in front of me and placed his large hands on my shoulders. I could feel the strength radiating from those hands, and it reassured me in some way. He spoke, almost as quietly as I had.

"Look to me, Levi."

I was so shocked by the way he addressed me, I forgot to be afraid for a moment. "How did you know my family and friends call me Levi instead of John?"

He smiled, and again I felt reassurance run through me.

"I told you, Levi, I know more about you than you most likely know about yourself. I know everything that pertains to you, all those whose lives had intersected with yours, everything since your birth."

Well, that was a bit of a gut-punch. It was then that I was informed about Gunther Spieglemann, and his demise. Caelius told me things about myself from my youth that I had forgotten even happened. He spoke for some time, detailing tiny things about me that I *knew* no one else on earth knew about. Finally, he fell silent and simply sat there, his large frame knelt in front of me in my chair, looking into my eyes. When I could speak again, I asked the only question that came to mind.

"Are you God?"

Caelius' eyes widened in surprise, and the next thing I knew, he was rolling, and I mean literally *rolling* on the floor, laughing so hard he was having a hard time even trying to answer me.

"I guess not, huh?" I mumbled.

Caelius sat up and caught his breath enough to talk to me, although he was prone over the next several minutes of breaking into giggles like a schoolgirl.

"No, Levi, I most certainly *not* God. Although ironically enough my name is a derivative of the Latin word for 'heaven'."

"Okay, so you're an angel, then?"

"No, again. I am just as human as you are."

"Right. I meet humans that are almost two thousand years old all the time. Hell, I think my librarian back home was closer to three thousand."

"And this librarian met a fatal injury and returned completely healed?"

"Well, no. All right, what are you?"

"*We*, Levi, what are *we*?"

I looked at him, thunderstruck. "How in the hell should *I* know?!?"

Caelius smiled again. "No, I was simply correcting your grammar. For what I am, you are, and vice versa."

"All right, then what are *we*, then?"

Caelius sat with his massive arms wrapped around his knees and paused before answering.

"I assume you are a Christian?" he asked.

"Yeah, what of it? I mean, I don't make it to church every Sunday, but I'm a Christian. Hey, wait a minute, you Romans fed Christians to *lions*, didn't you? Assholes."

Caelius shook his head. "Yes, it is true that Christians were crucified, forced to fight wild animals, burned, and all other manner of things in the arenas. But you forget. I died long before Rome had even heard of the man you call Jesus. So please save your indignation for a Roman that deserves it. Nero, perhaps. But not I. I killed for Rome. I cannot even begin to count those I sent to the afterlife in the name of the Empire. I also ordered the sacking and destruction of entire villages. There is more blood on my hands that can ever be washed away, but I had nothing to do with you Christians. I asked merely as a point of reference, so I can explain things to you."

"All right, I'm all ears. Explain away."

He took a deep breath (although he did it only so he could speak. I think I mentioned we don't have to breathe) and began.

"Whatever your religious belief system, you must set it aside for the moment, because what I am about to tell you will not fit into it anywhere. I have read your Bible, many times. I was there when some of it was being written, to tell the truth. And while some of it makes no sense at all, much of it seems to be good, common sense and decency. I speak now of the New Testament, not the Old. What you call the Old Testament has been around far longer than I. The Old Testament was written by ancient Israelites, and is a fairly blood-thirsty affair.

However, the New Testament, the teachings of the one called Jesus of Nazareth, these seemed to be very calm, for the time. 'Turn the other cheek'? No one had ever even thought of such a thing before. But I digress. What is important here is that you place what you believe to the side. I know not if your religion is correct or mine is, or any of the hundreds of others. I know only this: no matter what form God may take, the Fates exist. Do you know of the Fates?"

I had to think about it for a moment. I had read about them in school, but it was a dim memory. "Yeah, I sort of remember them… well, not very much, to tell the truth."

Caelius shook his head and muttered "Uneducated plebeians" before he took up his narrative again.

"The Fates were yet another thing Rome took from Greece. In Ancient Greek, the Fates were called Moirai, we Romans called them the Moerae. There were three Moerae: Clotho, Lachesis, and Atropos. The thread of man's life was in their hands. From birth to death, they controlled his destiny. Clotho was the spinner of the thread, Lachesis was the allotter of the length of the thread, and Atropos was the known as the 'unturnable', for when she decided the thread was to be cut, cut it was. No man could sway her. The mighty Julius Caesar was as unable to stay her hand as was the lowliest beggar in the streets."

"Now, it was believed that the Moerae were infallible. They could make no errors, no mistakes. Theirs was divine judgment and was perfection. And for the most part… this is true."

I stopped him there. "Pardon? For the most part? Seems to me that a job as important as that would require some pretty strict quality control."

Caelius' eyes snapped to mine and burned with anger. His voice was low and menacing when he spoke. "In all of time, of all the billions upon billions of human lives that have passed through the hands of the Moerae, there have been twenty-six 'mistakes', if you wish to call them that. Do you not think this to be an impressive bit of 'quality control', Levi?"

I was taken aback by his anger and held up my hands in a placating manner. "I apologize, Caelius. I was unaware you were close personal friends with the Fates. What the hell?"

With visible effort, he calmed himself. "Actually, I would not call myself close and personal friends of the Moerae. I would call myself their employee. Just as you will."

Well. That's interesting, I thought. Out loud, I said, "I have an employer Caelius. Her name is the United States Army, and she is *very* jealous of her employees moonlighting."

Caelius flapped a hand dismissively at me. "Your employment for the army of your country ended in France two hours and sixteen minutes ago, when you were killed in action whilst storming Omaha Beach. You were one of four thousand, four hundred and fourteen men killed taking the beaches."

My jaw dropped. "Four *thousand?* We lost four *thousand?* My God!"

Caelius' eyes took that cold cast again. "No, you lost four thousand, four hundred and fourteen. Those were just the killed. The wounded were much, much greater in number. You forget, boy, I lost twenty thousand men around me in three days. Not wounded, dead. *Slaughtered.* So, forgive me if I don't grow misty-eyed at your losses."

I was moving before I knew I had even given it thought. Caelius was still sitting in front of my chair, and although he outweighed me by almost seventy pounds or so and towered over me by almost eight inches, I had something he didn't. Rage. These were my friends he was talking about like they were pawns on a chessboard. I hit him with a flying tackle and we rolled all the way across the floor and into the (fortunately) unlit fireplace. I didn't have any fucking *strategy*, either, I'll tell you that. I was just going to beat his eyes out of his head.

The initial rage faded rather quickly, and I was surprised to find myself with Caelius held off the floor by his throat. He was bleeding from both nostrils, his mouth, his eyes were both blackening even as I watched, and blood was pouring down the left side of his neck from a head wound I couldn't see. I slowly lowered him to the floor (realizing as I did that he seemed to weigh nothing at all), and stepped away slowly until I was as far from him as I could get in the room.

"Caelius…" I began. He held up his hand for silence.

As I watched, he brushed the dirt from his clothing. The blood had stopped flowing from every wound and his bruises disappeared as

I looked on. He twisted his head from side to side, popping his neck and stretched his arms above his head. Within a few seconds, he looked as dapper and put together as he had when I had first seen him. Looking down at myself, I saw there was not as much as a rip in my suit. "Caelius…" I tried again, but he simply raised his hand again.

"Nefertari told me that the newest of us are the strongest. I seemed to have forgotten that. I thank you for reminding me. It is… unusual to feel pain. I have not felt any since my time with Nefertari, and that was a very, very long time ago." He looked into my eyes. "I ask you your forgiveness. I made light of the death of friends, and that was not seemly of me. Do I have your forgiveness?"

I nodded slowly. "Caelius, what just happened?"

He smiled slightly. "It appears that I offended you, and you took umbrage with that and thrashed me soundly. Or did I miss something? I must admit, you move so fast it is difficult to keep up."

"*I* thrashed *you*? Uh…*how?*"

"By using your hands and feet, and at one point, I *think* you used your head, to pummel me until you were finished. Again, I deserved it, and it has served me well, both as a lesson in manners and as a lesson in humility. It is easy to forget that you are not impervious to pain when it happens so very rarely."

My head was reeling. "You said I was moving so fast it was hard to keep up. What does that mean? I was moving at usual speed. I mean, maybe a *little* faster than that, because I was pissed, but not so fast you couldn't have seen me. And how did you let me get the best of you? I'm just a grunt, you're a nearly two thousand year-old Roman officer with God knows how much training. You should have mopped the floor with me. Just look at you! You're almost twice my size!"

Caelius smiled at me and said "Do you always judge your adversary by his size? For that matter, did your army not drop small groups of what you call "Airborne" soldiers from the night sky into France before the invasion? And did not these small groups work effectively against a much larger force, disrupting their attempts to defend the beaches?"

I shook my head. "Caelius, I don't know how well the 101st boys did. I was in the water, remember? Although I hope like hell you're right. I hope the Airborne guys raised pure hell with the Krauts while we were hitting those beaches."

Caelius smiled again. "The "101ˢᵗ boys", as you put it, did indeed "raise pure hell with the Krauts". The original drops were scattered, and things did not go as planned, as is often the case once battle begins, but the men on the ground came together admirably and were able to do far more than their part in this contest." He stopped for a moment and looked at me closely. When he resumed, there was a slight edge to his voice. "You do realize, I hope, that I have a fervent desire to see your forces win this war, do you not?"

I was taken aback again. Caelius seemed to have that effect on me. After a pause, I said, "Well, sure, I figure you want us to whip them. Every red-blooded American wants..." I stopped. Caelius said nothing, just stood waiting for me to continue. It had finally hit me. There was a slight tremor in my voice as I said, "You're not a red-blooded American, are you? If everything you've told me is true, and I'm beginning to believe it is, you're a... well, a red-blooded Roman, I suppose. That said, I don't really see why the hell you care one way or another about this war. I mean, you work for the Fates, are almost two thousand years old…why the hell *would* you care about just another war that has nothing to do with you?" Another light bulb went off. "Shit! You're a Roman! That means you're a goddamn Italian, right? You *do* realize we're kicking the hell out your country too, right?"

Caelius smiled again. "Yes, Levi, I am aware your country is at war with what used to be mine. I must stress the word "used". The Roman Empire was not simply Italy, as I am sure you understand. What I meant was that I have a very… shall we say…*personal,* interest in your country defeating the Axis."

"Why?" I asked. "Why would you want Italy defeated by anyone?"

"Not Italy, Levi. Italy is not Rome. I wish you to defeat *Germany*, and soundly."

"Okay, I'm confused. It's official. What are you talking about?"

Caelius took a deep breath and said, "Do you not recall where I told you I died?"

I took a second to recall the story he had told me earlier. "You were killed in the Teutoburg Forest, you said. Fighting under General Varus."

"Yes, and *where* is the Teutoburg Forest?"

"Uh…Germania?" I asked hesitantly.

"Yes… Germania. And where is this fool Adolph Hitler running this war?"

I probably looked as stupid as I felt. "Germany. Germania. You're talking about the same people, aren't you? So, you mean that the same people that killed you and your men almost two thousand years ago are shooting at my friends right now?"

Caelius grinned. "Well, not the *exact* same people, since they have been dead for a very long time, but their descendants, certainly."

I shook my head. "Jesus. We're fighting the same people that killed you that long ago. I can't get my head around that."

"Time is a wheel, Levi. Things are circular, and always will be. This is how this world works, and you must come to grips with this, and soon."

We spent the rest of that day talking. I remember draining the bottle of whiskey and being furious that it had absolutely no effect on me, and that from now on, it never would. I learned that I was breathing only as a learned reflex, something that messed with my head in a major way when I just stopped breathing for over an hour, which Caelius timed, to prove that I no longer needed to. I learned that I was still able to feel all the longings and passions of humanity, but that I no longer actually needed any of them to survive. In fact, I needed nothing whatsoever to survive. And nothing could destroy the body I inhabited. Shoot me, stab me, set me on fire, drown me... I'd just stand up, brush myself off and kick your ass for you. Caelius warned me that having that sort of power could be addictive, and I had to be certain that I never abused it. The normal ebb and flow of mortals could not be effected by what we were. Much like the vampires I mentioned earlier, our existence had to remain totally secret. All of which brought me to the final, ultimate question.

"So, we're immortal, invincible, and can't get drunk. Great. What the hell *are* we, Caelius?"

"I've told you, Levi. We are the operatives of the Fates."

"And that means what, exactly?"

"We serve to retain the balance between the world of mortals and that of… Others."

"What the hell do you mean, "*Others*"? You mean like men from Mars or something?"

"No, not men from Mars, you fool. There is a thin fabric between the world of mortals and a realm of things that you will unfortunately have learn to deal with, and soon."

"Right. So you expect me to believe that we're the immortal cops or something, and we have to stand watch over this "fabric" you're talking about. Is that about right?"

Caelius looked at me sadly and said, "Yes, Levi, that's just about a perfect definition of what we are."

I sat back down in the chair with my head in my hands to process all this. Caelius was patient, and merely stood looking out his windows at Central Park.

Suddenly it hit me. I bolted upright from the seat and whipped around to look at Caelius, only to find he'd done one of those high-speed shuffles and was now sitting at his desk. Impatiently, I turned to him and opened my mouth to speak.

"So", he said, "you've finally gotten around to asking how, exactly, this happened to you. Am I correct?"

"Are you reading my mind? Because if you are, just fucking quit it, right now." I was a bit steamed at this point. But Caelius just took it in stride, that little half-smile on the corner of his mouth. When he spoke again, he voice remained calm.

"No, I'm not reading your mind, Levi. In fact, my ability to do that ended the second you were killed in France. Your mind is a blank wall to me now. But to answer your question in a more civil manner than which it was asked, I knew what you were thinking because I had that same look on my face almost two thousand years ago, when the proverbial "light bulb" went off in my head. That's all. I recognize the signs."

"All right, big guy, if you know my question, seems like that you should know the answer to it."

Caelius smiled again, a full smile that lit up his face. "I do know the answer, but there is someone much better versed in this line of questioning than I to answer. In fact, I believe she is here now."

I was now totally confused. There was no one in the room but the two of us, and yet Caelius looked expectantly, not at the door, but the couch across the room from my chair. *That's it,* I thought, *if he starts talking to the damned furniture, I'm outta here. End of story."* I turned towards the couch for a second, then back to Caelius. Something in the corner of my eye made me look back, and I was just in time to see the purest white mist departing, leaving behind the most beautiful woman I had ever seen.

She had skin that was somehow the color of café-au lait, and yet shimmered gold in the light. Her hair was jet, black, and fell past her shoulders and all the way down her back. Her eyes were pools of warm onyx, somehow totally black, and yet completely able to show every possible emotion. Her face…my god, her face…and her body…I have to stop. Needless to say, this was the first time the full force of my sex drive kicked in since I'd been shot in the head, and brother, let me tell you…it kicked in *hard.*

Caelius had respectfully rose, and turned his hand to our visitor. "Levi Johnson, Private First Class, Serial Number 273-88-7868, please meet Nefertari. She is an Egyptian, as I'm sure you can tell, and is several thousand years older than I."

I couldn't make my mouth move, as hard as I tried. Fortunately for my, Nefertari was there to pick up the slack. When she spoke…well, let's just say her voice matched the rest of her just fine. A slight accent, but I can tell you, I would listen to this woman read laundry lists for weeks, just to hear her talk.

"Caelius, have you yet to learn manners? You do not speak of a woman's age! It is forbidden!"

Caelius came around the desk, and suddenly, he was holding one of the most beautiful flowers I have ever seen. I just had no idea where he had gotten it from, because I could have sworn it was not in his hand when he stood up. He gave Nefertari the flower and said, "Your favorite, unless things have changed drastically over the last 450 years."

Nefertari took the flower and held it to her face with a warm smile. "The Blue Lotus. And yes, Caelius, it is still my favorite, although it would have been all the sweeter if you had actually had it here and not just manifested it. But it is the thought that counts. How have you been, *merwet?*"

Caelius came close to blushing before his Roman calm took over. "Nothing new to report, *amica mea,* things have been extraordinarily quiet of late. I have seen nothing for nearly a century."

Nefertari shook her head, her hair moving like the ripples of a pond. I was struck all over again at her beauty. I suddenly realized that the cut of the dress pants I was wearing were not going to cover my embarrassment in the least when she looked my way. But then she turned to me and suddenly there was no passion on my part. My groin may as well been on the far side of the moon. She smiled at me and said in a soft voice, "Levi Johnson, Private First Class, Serial Number 373-88-7868. That is a very long name. Are all the men of your village named thusly?"

It felt like she was making fun of me somehow, so I quipped right back, "Ma'am, in the town of Bluejacket, out of the 2300 people that live there, there were five hundred, sixty-eight men that volunteered and are now named like me. That's almost a quarter of the town. So, a fairly good portion of my 'village is named thusly'. Ma'am."

I heard Caelius give off a soft growl and could sense him tensing to spring at me. Well, the lady *had* asked. And if Caelius decided that he was going to pounce on me, I'd thump him again. I would hate to do that in the presence of a lady, but if he bought it, he'd have to drive it home. But before any more fireworks erupted from Caelius, Nefertari held up one slender hand and said softly "Peace, Caelius. Have not two thousand years taught you any patience at all?"

It was a very odd sight to see a huge man dip his head and shuffle his feet like a schoolboy in the face of a woman that *might* have been five feet tall in sandals. But shuffle he did. And he muttered something under his breath about it "being a trying week". Right. I spent a sleepless night aboard a naval vessel, threw up all over my boots in a Higgins boat, and then got my head blown off in the ocean off of France a few hours ago, and *he's* had a trying week.

Nefertari looked back at me and smiled. I would have gleefully murdered kittens for her if she had asked. *That's* how incredible she looked. She said, "I merely meant by what name would you feel most comfortable with me addressing you. There was no disrespect intended, I assure you."

I grinned shyly back. I was beginning to see how Caelius felt. "Ma'am, you can call me whatever you want, but my friends call me Levi."

"A pact, then. I shall henceforth call you Levi, but only if you agree to never again use the word 'Ma'am' in reference to me, but instead call me Nefertari." She paused for a moment. "Perhaps later, when we have grown better acquainted, you may use the name my close companions have for me .Do you agree to my terms?"

It took me a second to work all that out. Both Caelius and Nefertari's English was perfect, but it was so formal that it almost sounded foreign to me. Of course, Army life isn't known for producing many Walt Whitmans. Once I had deciphered it, I said, "Yes, I agree. You're Nefertari and I'm Levi, and the angry Roman in the corner is Caelius." I glanced over at him, only to find him grinning broadly. I was beginning to think he might have been a bit schizophrenic.

Nefertari held her arms out to me, and I hesitantly embraced her. She was soft and warm and a woman, and I once again found myself wishing for my battle fatigues, which were much looser and could hide any number of things, an erection among them. She noticed, not that she could help it, but embraced me anyway, and then stepped back as if nothing had happened. But as she assumed her place on the couch, she shot me the tiniest glance from under her eyelashes and the ghost of a grin. I took my seat in a very expeditious manner, crossing my legs and smiling politely.

Caelius coughed slightly to bring things back to order and Nefertari nodded her head slightly. Looking at me, she said, "Levi, you were alive when you awoke this morning, died this day, and yet here you sit now. Do you accept this to be true?" I nodded, not knowing what else to say. She continued. "Caelius has explained what has occurred, has he not?" I nodded again. "Good. The one thing that he has left out of his explanation is exactly how this has come to pass. He has explained that the Fates have cut your life line, only to have that cutting fail. I am here to explain how that has happened, and why."

I inhaled, out of habit, not realized I hadn't drawn a breath since our embrace. It's amazing how fast you get used to not doing the simple things, like breathing. I gave her a thankful look and said,

"'Nefertari, you have *no* idea how much I would appreciate that."

Nefertari sat back on the couch, much as Caelius had earlier,

took a deep breath, and began.

"Since the beginning of mankind, the Moerae, to use Caelius'

term, have been charged with a single purpose: to measure out the

length of human life. Caelius has explained this to you already, so I will

not go over ground already covered. This system, set in place by a

being or beings that we humans have taken to calling gods (albeit by

different names), has worked to near perfection for eons. Then, one

day nearly a hundred thousand years ago, there was an event that shook

the very foundations of space, time, and reality. As allotted, the time of

a man's life ran out. As the Moerae you know as Atropos cut the cord,

something happened that had never occurred before. The thread of the

man's life severed, as it should, all save a single, hair-thin silver thread.

The man fell to his death off an ice cliff, and then found himself

standing in a forest thousands of miles from where he had just been.

This, I am sure, is a familiar story to you."

"This unfortunate soul found himself with powers he could not explain, and the curse of immortality. And yes, I see the question in your eyes, but believe me when I say to you that immortality will become a curse to you, just as it has to us all. All you love will wither and die, as will all that which you come to love in the future. If there is a Hell, then I often think this may be it, and we must be very wicked to deserve it. But then I think on what I have seen and fought, as you will, and I know that this is not Hell, but Paradise by comparison."

"But I digress. The man whose life thread could not be cut, and it is said every attempt was made to cut it, continued his travels, learning new skills and growing ever stronger. He came to believe he had become a god. With such power and longevity compared to the humans around him, it is hard to blame him for his misguided belief. He made his home in a vast valley near a river on the plains of what you now call Africa. Tribes would come from all points of the compass to meet this god they had heard of, and grow to worship him. This continued, unabated, for the next sixty-four thousand years, when suddenly into the village walked another man with the same powers as the first. This caused great consternation, as I am sure you can imagine. The stories tell that the second man came in peace, attempting only to find another like himself to share his experiences with. However this was not something the first man was interested in."

"The stories say the battle lasted for seven days, and at its conclusion, the entire valley had been lain to waste, and all who lived there were dead. Still the two immortals stood, not an injury upon them, just as strong as they were at the beginning of the contest."

"The second man viewed what the battle had caused with horror, and vowed never again to lay eyes upon the other until such a time as he could destroy him, for what had begun as a mission of peace had destroyed a population. The first man matched his threat, and foretold of a time when great demons would stand by his side, his servants and soldiers, to erase all trace of his opponent from the earth, which he said was his domain by right."

"I do not know how well versed you are in you are in your Bible, but should you research it and the Hebraic scrolls associated with it, you will find the names of these first two immortals. They feature heavily in the stories, although in the books, the order in which they appear in history is reversed."

I just shook my head. "I've been to church since I was a boy", I said, "but I didn't really pay all that much attention, to tell the truth. Mostly I sat in the back and blew spit wads at the other fellas, I'm afraid to say."

Nefertari shot a confused glance at Caelius, who just shook his head. Dismissing it, she continued.

"The name of the first immortal was Abbudoni, which was later translated into 'Abaddon'. The second immortal's name was Aelyin, which was also later changed, this time to 'Elyon'. Are either of these names significant to you?"

I thought hard for a few moments, but finally just shook my head and said, "Nefertari, I'm just a dumb grunt that didn't have the sense to stay out of the way of a bullet. You and Caelius are both talking way above my pay grade."

Again, she shot Caelius a look, and again she received a shake of the head. The whole thing felt like a test, and any moment they were both going to stand up and tell me I was not cut out for this, and I would find myself bobbing off France again. Instead, Nefertari just took another breath and continued.

"Levi, 'Abaddon' is Hebraic for 'Destroyer'. It is another way of saying 'Satan'. Conversely, 'Elyon' is Hebraic for 'Highest', which is one of the many facets of God. Do you see now?"

I sat in silence for a while, and when I spoke, my voice was devoid of emotion. "Well, if I'm understanding you right, the Bible has it all wrong…hell *all* the religions have it all wrong. God didn't created the Earth and then cast Satan out of heaven. Instead, Satan was here first, and God was some Johnny-Come-Lately to the party, right? About the only part anybody got right was that Satan is building an army to destroy everything. That sounds about right. Take everything good out of our spirituality, our faith, and leave nothing but the shit behind. Yeah, that sounds just about dead-on to me." I stood, looking at them. "Listen, I may not have been the best kid in Sunday School, but I will be damned if I'm going to play some sick game with you…whatever you are about God and the Devil. So, if it's the same to you, just stick me back on that fucking beach. I'd rather be fish bait with the back of my head gone than to live in the world you're describing."

Nefertari rose fluidly and placed her hands gently on my chest. She tilted her head up and looked deeply into my eyes. Her voice was earnest, quiet and sincere.

"No, Levi, you misunderstand. Abbudoni is no more Satan than I, nor is Aelyin God. They are simply the first of our kind, and through human error, they have been given these roles. Think on it. If you suddenly appeared to the men of your unit this instant, dressed as you are and simply walked up the beach, the bullets passing through you without harm, or you moved so quickly that you were at the top of the hill before the others could even make it ashore, what would they think of you?"

"Well, my First Sergeant would be yelling at me to stop fucking around and start killing some Germans, but the rest of the guys would be kind of spooked, I guess."

She smiled. "Exactly. Humans cannot understand what we are. Sometimes even *we* cannot understand what we are." This earned a grunt from Caelius. She shot him a quelling look. Returning to me, she said, "Levi, what we *are* is unimportant, as unbelievable as that might sound to you right now. It is what we *do* that is important. What I have told you about Abbudoni and Aelyin is true. Their war continues. But while Aelyin has sought enlightenment, truth, and justice for over fifty thousand years, Abbudoni has made good on his threat to enlist the vilest and evil creatures he can find to destroy Aelyin. It was Abbudoni that first found a way to punch through the fabric of this world and into the place of the Others, and he has been recruiting them ever since."

"In the last thirty thousand years, the Moerae have been unable to cut the life threads of just twenty-four humans. This day, you have made that number twenty-five. You are the first immortal to be created in over seven hundred years. Not counting Abbudoni, there are now twenty-six immortals that now roam this earth, righting that which has gone wrong, and setting the evil that Abbudoni, in his arrogance, has released here, back to the darkness from which it came."

She stepped closer. I could smell faint spices in her hair. Her voice was husky, barely a whisper, but filled with urgency. "Levi, your arrival has turned the tables on Abbudoni. With Aelyin's guidance, we now have the numbers to begin pushing Abbudoni's minions back, to bring light back to this world. And in time, we can defeat the megalomaniac himself, and forever close the portals between worlds, as it was meant to be. But we *need* you. The youngest of us are always the strongest, and for the next several thousand years, you will be able to easily defeat anything Abbudoni tries to send your way. You are the weapon we have been waiting for for so very long."

Nefertari stepped away, just a lingering trace of jasmine and cloves. She walked back to the couch and sat down. As Caelius hadn't moved from his seat, I felt uncomfortable standing alone, so I took my own seat. I sat with my elbows on my knees, deep in thought. There were more questions than I had room for answers, so finally I just looked up at them and said, "So, I'm just a weapon, huh?" Nefertari started to speak, but I raised my hand to silence her. "No, it's all right. I'm used to it. I *am* a weapon. U.S. General Issue, Private First Class, Serial Number 373-88-7868. My rifle has a serial number on it, too, but it's just an extension of weapon carrying it. They turned us *all* into weapons. I was a weapon for them in Tunisia back in February of last year. We got our asses handed to us at the Kasserine Pass. I lost a lot of good weapons there. Back home, they didn't call them that, or tell their serial numbers...back home they had names. I killed some German weapons there, too. I bet they had serial numbers that their folks back home never called them by, either. But you're right, I'm just a weapon. Been one since 1941. So, what difference does it make, right? I mean, what difference does it make whether I'm a weapon for the U.S. Army or this Aelyin or the Moerae, or God, or…whatever. A weapon is designed to be used in war, and from what you've said, this is a war, and an almighty big one, from the sound of it. So, use me. Tell me who I'm supposed to kill and I'll kill them. Why not?" I sat back, my head cocked toward the ceiling and for the first time noticed that it was a perfect reproduction of "The Creation of Adam" by Michelangelo. I burst out laughing at the irony.

Nefertari was kneeling before me in that creepy instantaneous way she and Caelius…and I guess *I* have. Her hands were warm on mine. "Oh, Levi, you are so much more than that. So very much more. In time, you will see."

And that is how I became the twenty-sixth member of a group of immortals that spend our time keeping the things you're afraid of under the bed from actually getting you. Nefertari was right, time did give me some perspective. As I stand here on this balcony in New York City in the year 2014, drinking a totally useless glass of Scotch (I may not be able to get drunk, but I can still enjoy the taste, thank you very much), and watching the surge of humanity below me, I marvel at how much has changed, and how quickly it seemed to do it.

In the summer of 1946, the thought of men on the moon was the stuff of comic books. In the summer of 2014, there are children below me right now with complex gadgets and electronic toys that my friends would have thought *came* from outer space. I can just imagine telling my old First Sergeant that in less than a hundred years, they would have cars that could run on corn. He would have laughed, and then knocked my face in for wasting is time.

No, Caelius had it right, too. Time is a wheel. I've noticed that wheels have a tendency to run you over if you're not watching. But I've found that the trick is to stand *inside* the wheel, and let it take you along for the ride. That's what I try to do. Well, that, and fight and kill things that would give you nightmares for the rest of your life. It's all right. I do it so you don't have to.

That's right, that's not the end of this tale, only this chapter. I've got more stories to tell than you have time to hear them. And I mean that literally. You would grow old and die before I could tell them all. Byproduct of immortality. Sorry about that. But just because I can't tell you all my stories doesn't mean I can't tell you a few of the juiciest ones. And I will, believe me, I will.

My name is Johnathon Levi Anderson, Levi to my friends, and I am one of the Keepers of the Light, or just Keepers for short. This morning I saved New York City from a Fire Demon about six times bigger than the Statue of Liberty, and not one person saw me do it.

What did you do today?

Ryan S. Pack was born and raised in Eastern Kentucky. He lives there still with his wife LuAnn and their four children. He was an Emergency Medical Technician for fifteen years before an injury ended that career. He has since spent his time in and out of college, where he remains one credit shy of a degree, and writing what he refers to as "My Ramblings". The Long Way Around is his first collection of short stories.